A baby boomer, raised at the beach in Southern California, and then later, as a high-school youth in the citrus groves of Ventura County slightly to the north, Dominic M. Martin was raised by diligent, demanding, and fun-loving parents who taught him that 'A man's words is his bond', and 'Always to give a 100% effort in all things'. These whimsical and keenly written stories, wrestled from the past, reflect those values inherited from those excellent parents.

To my parents, two of the very best.

Dominic M. Martin

NOVE

Nine Nicked and Negligent Tales
Taken from Mercury

AUSTIN MACAULEY PUBLISHERS™
LONDON • CAMBRIDGE • NEW YORK • SHARJAH

Ordering Information
Quantity sales: Special discounts are available on quantity purchases by corporations, associations, and others. For details, contact the publisher at the address below.

Publisher's Cataloging-in-Publication data
Martin, Dominic M.
Nove

ISBN 9798889101307 (Paperback)
ISBN 9798889101314 (ePub e-book)

Library of Congress Control Number: 2024909872

www.austinmacauley.com/us

First Published 2024
Austin Macauley Publishers LLC
40 Wall Street, 33rd Floor, Suite 3302
New York, NY 10005
USA

mail-usa@austinmacauley.com
+1 (646) 5125767

I would like to acknowledge Villanova Preparatory School in Ojai, California, its encouragement of free debate, logical thought, and muscular Christianity, and in particular, three rigorous Augustinian priests who taught me there: Jerome Bevilacqua O.S.A., Thomas J. McLaughlin O.S.A., and John P. Pejza O.S.A.

Table of Contents

Nota bene: Mercury was the patron of travelers and also of rogues, vagabonds, and thieves.

Hence, with the subtitle, the name of this Roman god is used to denote both a messenger and a thief.[1]

---

[1] From Brewer's Dictionary of Phrase and Fable. Revised Edition by Ivor H. Evans. Cassell Publishers Ltd. London. 1988. P. 729

Preface

All prefaces must contain scarcely more than two thoughts:

1. I cannot remember my childhood for sure since there is that persistent idea of mis-recalling, and
2. If, by chance, some small nibble of a story is true, it becomes a waystation or refuge: To counter or refute what otherwise might have been.

All these stories were 'nicked' since they were swiped, stolen, lifted, pilfered out of the past, which is never, of course, truly gone. One looks for a brief time at Time and walks away from her with a few rubrics, rubles, rubies. After all: Why do we bring back to our reclining minds this retrieved scrap or tidbit and not that one?

And don't we all falsify in the retelling, eagerly stretching the truth here, exaggerating shamelessly there? Of course, we do, of course. That explains the word 'negligent' in the subtitle. These stories emerge, based upon those headlong, more innocent days of a long-past blond youth, a lad not besmirched, a tadpole boy with no real or imagined ailments, tended to by most loving parents, dogged by not even a mirage of disappointment. Given the stories' transmutations, and their necessary emphasis of this over that, in those selections, these tales must be negligent fictions, that is, they must be rift with carelessness and neglect.

However, why do we so transpose and freeze, falsely, like a tipping camera might, one frame over another? Why? Because that is the way our memory works: We make a new room. We must mislead. We invent the story, to make the better tale. We invariably transform the facts and circumstance, the mood and the color of a scene, since we are not able, ever, to tell the truth, that is, of course, the whole truth, with no clouded omissions or shaded areas. So, we lie; we tell negligent lies. It is simply in our nature to do so. It would not be possible for us to do otherwise.

A Note on Nine[2]

NINE: Nine, five, and three are mystical numbers that have come down to us from the ages. Those three numbers are the diapason, the diapente, and the diatrion of the Greeks. Nine consists of a trinity of trinities. According to the Pythagoreans, man is a full chord, or eight notes, and deity comes next. Three, being the trinity, represents a perfect unity; twice three is the perfect dual, and thrice three is the perfect plural. This explains why nine is a mystical number.

For our purposes here, the most apt allusion is taken from Milton; that is, when the fallen angels were cast out of heaven. Milton writes,

"Nine days they fell." (Paradise Lost VI, 871).

---

[2] Material is taken from Brewer's, page 786.

As a kid, I remember looking southwest across the basin of Los Angeles from my friend Regan's house. Even though it was early morning that summer in August, you could see the smoke shifting across the pale blue sky, dirtying the sky's natural blue to a kind of unwashed tan. Or was it mauve? The riots in Watts just to the south of the city had commenced a few nights ago. It would take many days of the hot Santa Ana winds to make the sky clean again.

Burt and Mary

The Mahony family, husband and wife, lived across the street from us in a small, oak-floored house that must have been built right before World War II, just before the attack on Pearl Harbor, back in those distant days when we were pretty much all flush. After the war if a guy ventured into our neighborhood in the fifties, when I first did, the first thing he would notice was the bright pink color of the house. Burt, a house painter, wanted it that way to please his wife, Mary, since he would occasionally remark to her that the color of the house precisely matched that of her cheeks. I bet that their house had only two bedrooms, although one can never be sure. In front of the house, toward the street, a field of always trimmed and tended geraniums, a plot near the size of a full piece of plywood, filled the iodine beach air around it with its own, startling scent. Above it, poised like a resolute sentry, as if standing watch, was the window, my window, one which over the years I would consider my childish duty and obligation to attack and destroy.

The Mahoney's house, much to their eventual chagrin, was positioned at the bottom of a steeply descending alley. Empty alleys, back streets, narrow passageways, scattered lanes, or what the Italians call 'vicoli' were common in our neighborhood then because cars, back when these homes were constructed, had not yet taken over or seized the nation's consciousness. So, my buddies and I would play baseball, especially in the vacant alleys. Cars were hardly a thought, and many families did not own one. Instead, folks walked to work, took a bus, or rode the 'Red Car' trains that circumscribed the city, if they wanted to go to the heart of the spreading metropolis of Los Angeles some twenty miles away to the northeast. That is where I was born, or so I have been told, near the meager trickle coming out of the San Gabriel Mountains that is even today called the Los Angeles River.

I have discovered that one must learn to trust such information, not to quiz it or fritter much. Then, and down to today, Saint Vincent's Hospital, the first hospital in the city, stood at the busy intersection of 3rd Street and Alvarado Street, and nearly all of us children were born there since that is where our mother worked as a surgical nurse. She knew a doctor there, Dr. Worgen, who treated her gently, and to whom, every year, fully pregnant, distended, and plump, she would return to await his coaxing and deft ministrations for delivery of the new baby.

Here, now, upon the sky's blue, two new flags, le bandiere, emerge to flap about in the wind. They deserve our focused attention, or at least one may deem it so. Linking images can appear to create a greater thought or diverging resonance. To wit: Back then, on the night of September 30, 1951, I, still inside my mommy's tummy, had entered Saint Vincent's. So, too, though I did not know it, Pauline Pfeiffer, Ernest Hemingway's second wife, but long ago divorced from the famous writer, had entered the same hospital, complaining of terrible abdominal pain. On that day, Pauline was only 56 years old, which is far too young to die. A few hours earlier her ex-husband had called from his Finca Vigia hacienda just outside Habana, Cuba, to her son, Gregory's home, rousing in him much disquieted emotion. His mother would not see the next dawn, dying on the operating table on the first day of October from a pheochromocytoma tumor of one of her adrenal glands.

At exactly that same time, I would have been on another floor, the one for births, not for emergency surgeries. If my mom had not been busy dealing with me, she might have handed the scalpel or forceps to the surgeon working on her, trying valiantly to save Mrs. Hemingway. I knew that she had been the mother of two of his three sons, Patrick and Gregory. Patrick was so named for Patrick Murphy, the first of the two Murphy boys, scions of Sara and Gerald, to pass that name on. Pauline and Ernest, still married in February 1935, had visited the dying 12-year-old Patrick in Saranac Lake, New York, that day, and the sight of a child's life about to be unexpectedly extinguished made the big, tough Ernest cry.

Too, it, this story, reminds me of what George Joyce, James' little brother, sick and frail, on his deathbed said to the writer,

"I am too young to die."

That took place in North Dublin in what we would call a ghetto, another Italian word, or what some would term a slum. Exactly seventy years after George had died in 1902 at the age of fourteen and also on a Sunday, I stood in that same, still dirty, and unkempt yard, it covered with weak patches of yellow grass, and littered with mounds of dog feces. Aged twenty, I stood there with Ken Monaghan, the last surviving nephew of James Joyce, as he explained to me the mounting financial disaster that had beset the Joyce family.

He detailed how the fortunes of the Joyces declined steadily during the writer's childhood, as the family moved from prosperous Bray in the south part of the city to Dublin's dim north end. Mr. Monaghan explained to me that it, this northern section of Dublin, was at that time the worst slump in Europe.

So many connections, so many interlaced threads. Death joins with life, the famous with the unknown, the collision of time and place for subtle, ironic effect, across thousands of miles, hundreds of years. Hospitals are full of life and death, the incipiency of nascent and pesky cancer's urge to rise and kill the patient. No one goes there if he is well. My uncle who was also a brilliant doctor used to tell me that the easiest way to make a healthy man become quite ill was to have him visit his sick wife in hospital. Germs move through the air, and we cannot see them, no matter how hard we squint. To fight the invisible microbial world, all we can do is wash our hands and brush our teeth often.

Still, I would be doing neither for a dawdle since I was just born at 8pm that night and in my pudgy hands I could hold neither a toothbrush nor a bar of soap. Ernest, three hours later, which would have been in the middle of the night in Cuba, would learn the details of his second wife's passing, with all the technical clinical nuances, and feel grief, remorse, and sadness, and perhaps relive one more time his own betrayal of her with his third wife, Martha Gellhorn. However, all of that would take time to flourish, to be fed, one must guess, by copious digestion of rum drinks made from sugar cane, Cuba's largest crop. Blood: It never goes away. I remember Old William's saw that the past is not dead; it is not even past. It is eight o'clock at night now, and my mother is exhausted, now that the jet plane, me, I, io, just out of the hanger has landed, pink and squealing onto the deck of the carrier. My father had come to visit, but I cannot see him because my eyes are tentative, clouded, wrinkled. There is only so much one can say to a crying baby. And it is far too early to place any bets. Will I be an athlete or champion? Even now, across oceans of time, I can smell his acrid, armpit onion smell. And, my mother, she was deeply asleep, probably given a strong sedative, some sleep-inducing drug so that she might rest until dawn. My father would have had a tedious 21-mile-long drive home, traveling only by surface streets, snaking his way southwest, to reach our beach house in Manhattan Beach, but before making the long drive, he would have driven over to Phillipe's, the nearby home of the French Dip sandwich. Of this there can be no doubt. He would have had the lamb version of the famous sandwich, since it is quite rare, and some beets and pickles, and a couple of beers, lager, since that was the only beer men drank back then. And when he got home, after saying goodnight to my brother and tucking him in to bed, he would have had a couple of shots of the Irish to steady his nerves, to calm himself for sleep. Before joining it, he would have made a prayer of thanksgiving, happy that all in his small family was healthy, that none had turned out like Patrick or George or Pauline, all of whom are dead. Dad was happy that we were all alive and might live, live for another day, which would be tomorrow.

Back then, they kept mothers in hospital for longer. To watch and guard or churn for fees; however, it is not wise to so argue. So, we, Mom and I, stayed until the third of October when our second, coincidental flag planted high above soaring historic events began to flap about in the ocean's daily breeze. For, when we arrived home (it was my first time to smell the sea, to feel the salt on my skin, to sniff the sea's brine and iodine in the buoyant coastal air), after all the hubbubs had died down (there's that word again), over the dinner table my father said to my mother,

"You should have seen what happened to Mantle today in the World Series' first game. A deep shot was hit to right-center. Mantle was steaming toward it like a train rolling through a station. At the last split second, DiMaggio in center says, 'I got it', and catches the ball. At the same instant, Mantle pulls up sharply and steps onto some kind of drainage culvert, blowing out his knee. The young kid from Commerce, Oklahoma went down in a clump. He is in the hospital now. I hope he'll be able to play next year, but for certain he's done for the series."

My mother looked at him with mild derision, saying,

"I just spent a dozen hours in labor, and all you can think of is baseball. Baseball! Is that all men can think about? Sports?"

Pretty much, and I counter: Why not? As I grew up in that crowded neighborhood so close to the sea, there was always some sort of game, but, usually, it was baseball. Why, I could stay outside within keen sight of our front door (whose weathered brass door handle, the one with the scalloped edges and considerable deep pitting due to the closeness of the sea, is still there, even today), and whenever I blew my heavy chromium whistle (one made in Ohio and never Japan, never mind the deceitful bastards), almost fifty kids would stream out of the various brightly colored houses. Half wore striped shirts, Converse tennis shoes, Jack Purcell sneakers, and thick Levis jeans, some with gaping holes in the knees. Huddling, expectant, ready to get going, we would quickly agree on a game, and it was usually baseball. Using anything as bases: Cans, sweaters, lumpy sweatshirts, extra gloves, we would, like ready soldiers, troop to the alley and begin to play, to lose ourselves in the game's frank cadence and esoteric customs, that is, to reach outside of all time and space. None of us ever thought that the window at the Mahoney's house, no, none of us ever thought it would be so easy to hit, and none of us ever recognized that the window's sheer size meant that it was almost asking for the ball.

Still, a small silver lining always exists, no matter what the silly conman says. The window, roughly four feet by twelve feet, was broken up into many (Were there sixty-four? Perhaps seventy-two?) panes of glass; so, if we were to hit a ball to it, into it, them, we could break only one or two, or, in the worst instance, three, we would not be able to break them all, since to do that would take a bomb or explosion, something like a missile or projectile from a gun or tank.

And besides, or so we baseball layers of the neighborhood figured, the co-owner of the house, Burt Mahoney, was a painter; and since he was a painter, he could replace a few panes easily enough. Of course, he could, we told each other as daft dingleberries, of course he could. Accounting for mullions and trim, sash and casings, each pane must have been ten inches square or perhaps eight, which was the same number as my age.

Nine would not have been possible since it is an odd number and a good one, too, one of the very best since it was also the number of my favorite player, Roger Maris, the Greek from Fargo, North Dakota, who played that very season, 1960, right field for the New York Yankees. I knew that his name originally was Maras. He nearly could have dated my mom since she was from North Dakota as well, from a miniature town called Hastings, a once prosperous burgh now nearly dried up and shrunken, but by then she was older and already married to my dad. Anyway, I was really an L.A. Dodgers fan. Had they really left Brooklyn for me? In those days, I thought so.

Thomas Davis and Frank Howard were new to the team that summer, and both were smacking the ball hard. And there was that other number nine, for Wally Moon; and I wondered: Would he hit .300? It would be close. Also, the aging Duke, Mr. Snider from nearby Compton, was having an off year, since he was often injured with cranky knees, and his batting average was terrible.

All of us would argue amongst ourselves: Would the Duke return to his prior glory, and would just-injured Carl Furillo, the Reading Rifle, do the same? How many of these ballplayers, once their stupendous talents had begun to slip, ebb, dissipate, would regain their prior fleeting glory, recapturing their tensile and sinewy youth?

One day that summer, I visited the Mahoney's house. For me, it was a little scary. I had been inside their house only a couple of times before. Mrs. Mahoney ("Call me Mary, will you, son?") was always baking things: Cookies, small cakes, what she called a Hungarian Christmas loaf, though it wasn't Christmas yet, and she was not Hungarian, but Irish. One more time I saw again that she had a bright pink face, almost red, since there must have been so much real red blood close to her skin, just underneath. Often, she would see my mom, or call, and say,

"Send that boy of yours over, will you, please! I've got a little something for you all."

So, I'd scamper over in my striped shirt, my Levis, and Jack Purcell sneakers, and as soon as I entered the shaded concealment of their home (they usually kept the drapes closed since the big window, the one whose 8 or 10 inch square panes we were about to start breaking, one by one, each at its own time, faced directly westwards toward the always bright afternoon sun gleaming there above the ocean, all the way up to the ceiling), I could smell the nutmeg, the cinnamon, the allspice, the dough. Fresh yeast smells from risen bread quickly filled my eight-year-old nostrils.

I thanked her for the gift, a pan of brownies full of nuts and extra chocolaty. And when I, as most lads do without even knowing it, stared, not looked, into her older Irish woman's face, I saw not the wrinkles about the eyes, nor the dark spots upon her temple, but again I noticed how pink her cheeks were. Pink. Again, I thought to myself: *Her cheeks are so full and fresh and pink because underneath the skin, her skin, there is nothing but blood, lots of red blood, red.*

And, before I left, I looked quickly at Burt. He was sixty spot-on but looked older since over the years he had been out in the sun a lot. He frightened me a little. Since it was an early fall Saturday around noon, he was watching the Notre Dame football game on television. He was yelling at the TV, loudly swearing at Coach Joe Kuharich. Mary said to Burt,

"Will you watch your mouth, please, Burt. Can't you see we have some young company here?"

Burt looked at me, or through me, since his bright blue Irish eyes did not seem to focus. Eventually, his eyes evened a little, and he smiled at me, so I could see his yellow or tan teeth, and he said to me,

"How are you doing, buddy? Want to watch the game for a little? ND is getting beat again. Nineteen sixty is not their year. Might be time to change the goddamn coach."

Mary frowned at Burt as I departed, having declined in a soft, scared voice to watch the game with Burt. And as I left with my still warm pan of brownies, so warm that they nearly hurt my hands, I noticed one more time that the Mahoney's house was pink, a bright pink, the kind of deep tropical color one might see in Culiacan or Mazatlán. I thought that the pink of the house precisely matched the pink of Mary's cheeks and that Burt, Mr. House Painter, must have picked out and painted that color on purpose because for close to fifty years, through all kinds of difficulties, long years of normal strife and financial anxiety and war-time confusion, he had loved her deeply and she, him.

* * *

Back then, in those days now so long ago, my best friend was Tom Crivelli. Actually, it was Tommasino Crivelli. His parents were from northern Italy, hailing from the region close to the Piave River where Ernest Hemingway, working for the Red Cross as a driver, had been shot on the dot forty-two years ago. I called him Tom, because it was a shorter name, and this was America. He was short and dark, and a very good athlete. Naturally, his favorite player on the Dodgers was the fellow Italian, Carl Furillo, who by that time had decided to retire due to an injury to his leg. Last year, 1959, when he still played right field for the Dodgers, Furillo, if the batter was lollygagging or dogging it just a little after a sharp single to right, would fling the ball quickly to Gil Hodges, throwing the guy out at first. No one does that anymore. All during that long summer, Tom had taught me plenty of words in Italian, so we used that language sometimes as a secret code, like boys do, so that our parents would not hear or understand what we were planning to do next.

And so it was that day in the early fall of 1960 that we marched, come soldati avidi, like committed soldiers, to the top of the alley and began to bat, to play baseball. We considered ourselves to be part of the crack core of the Italian army: The Arditi. The ardent. We were cocky and determined. We always played with a hardball since we figured that lumpy softballs, plastic wiffle balls, or tennis balls were only for sissies, ninnies, pansies, sissy shits, and none of us, to be sure, was one of those. Windows in the houses that surrounded us, and in the cars, and all kinds of other fragile things that might break were all around us, but we did not care about that one whit since it was time for a game, time to hit. And in the greatest danger was Mahoney's large window at the base of the alley, only a mere fifty yards away.

None of us thought the panes of the window would ever get broken. No. Such a bad thing would not be possible. We began.

So, just then, my buddy, Tom, pitched the dirty, scuffed hardball, a used one the color of a deer's back. Using my nicked and scratched-up Louisville Slugger bat, turning my hips just a split second before throwing my arms forward, that is, making my bellybutton immediately face the pitcher, Tom, I swung, hard. Upon contact, did you detect any smell of burning wood? As a keen student of baseball, I knew that Ted Williams used to ask that same question. Perhaps a trace? Just before contact of the bat to the ball, I had one searing thought: *Suddenly, bad things can happen at any time and unexpectedly.* For once that day, I hit the brown ball smack on the button, on the rare, sweet spot. I had made good and commendable contact, so much so that my arms stung for a moment, and the ball sailed upward, then still further upward in a broad and gathering arc, traveling down the alley's impossibly short length in less than a second. I cringed. The baseball bounced once in the middle of the street in front of the Mahoney's house, just dodging the Hudson family's crème-colored 1958 VW bug in a beautiful high curve, and then it crashed clear through one of the panes in the window. The hole the ball made was neat, in the broken windowpane's middle, and right afterward I could see inside that the Mahoney's curtain billowed a little past the glass due to the daily onshore breeze coming from the ocean.

Most of us scrambled, split, scattered; however, I knew I had better fess up and face the music. Tom went with me as a friend. Mary Mahoney opened the door and smiled at us. She said,

"Don't worry, boys. It is not the end of the world. Burt can fix it. Try and be more careful next time."

Considering ourselves very lucky to have met such a nice lady, yet neither knowing how to spell the word 'careful', nor what it meant, we left.

Over the remaining weeks of that 1960 summer and fall, as the nation braced for the November election, at a rate of one per week or thereabouts, we (using truthfully the Royal We since the damage was perpetrated by many of us baseball soldiers and not a few) broke six more of the Mahoney's windows, bringing the total to seven, which is Mickey's number. Each time, after just a few days, Burt would repair the window, re-glaze it, re-spackle it, re-prime it, re-paint it. Each time, we would apologize to Burt and Mary, and each time, they would say,

"Don't worry. We are just glad you can play ball."

We couldn't believe our luck: Such forgiving people.

But, that very night, after number seven was broken, though he did not know the total at the time, my dad gave me a stern order,

"You're not to play in the alley anymore, do you hear me? Cripes, there is a huge, open, green, and grassy field only three blocks to the south, at Robinson School! You have played the old gooseberry with him and not respected his property! You kids have all gotten fat and sassy! And you are to buy Burt a present of some sort since you dweebs, you inconsiderate whelps, you little numbskulls, have been such a royal pain-in-the-rear."

However, what would I purchase for this 60-year-old painter? I could not buy him a bottle of Irish Whiskey, even though I knew that he would like that very much, since I was too young to buy alcohol.

What was I to do? Then, I hit upon it: Perhaps I would buy a plastic model of a ship since I knew he liked to work with his hands, and like all the Irish, he loved the sea and ships, almost as much as he loved his wife, Mary.

The next Saturday morning, I walked half a mile downtown, which offered three different candy and hobby stores. Penny candy, hundreds of kinds, was displayed in open form so any crass and willful kid, someone like me, could grab a small brown bag and using my grimy hands like a shovel or backhoe, load up. One time from one of the stores, if truth be told, I stole some candy, which was easy to do since for some silly reason the cash register was in the back of the store, far from the front door. After that day, I was afraid of getting caught, and so I never did that again. Eventually the owners wised up and moved the cash register closer to the front door.

That store was my favorite. Too, it was across the street from a bakery where you could get jelly-filled, powdered sugar donuts as soon as they got out of the oven. The candy and hobby store had tons of models, models of ships, trains, cars, planes, helicopters, monsters, you name it. I remembered that my dad had told me once that Burt had been in the Navy for both wars, so I decided to purchase a ship for him. (I knew already that you only call it a boat if it is less than ten feet, or, at least, so mean cully says). Seeing that the store did not offer for sale many modern ships, for only 4.95 clams, I bought The Santa Maria, Cristofero Colombo's lead vessel from his first voyage in 1492. And, eager with the unasked-for-joy of all those that give something unique or special to another, I strode the short distance home.

I decided to give the small box containing The Santa Maria to Burt straight away since a real man would not want the present wrapped up in a bunch of frilly paper only meant for girls. By that time, it was Saturday morning, near 11:30 am. Walking past the plot of geraniums, whose scent again seemed to me to be almost made of pee or quinine, and even though I was afraid to do so, since the house was so very dark and quiet with all the shades drawn, I knocked. I heard a loud, coves voice bark,

"What the blazes!"

I heard stumbling noises, things falling to the oak floor, drinks being spilled. I thought to myself: *Perhaps a glass was broken?* Finally, the door opened, and through the screen, right away I could see Burt, but he was drunk, completely plastered, ebbro, and ubriaco. Those last two words were ones that Tom had taught me. Burt seemed angry, disconsolate. I thought he might yell at me, which would make me run away, but he did not. He said,

"Oh, it is you! How are you, you little scamp, whelp, rascal? Did you hear, fierce one, garang, that Notre Dame is losing again? That leadsman Kuharich must go! You want to watch the game with me? It's in South Bend. What's up, high pockets? Landlubber? Button it, will you, welsher? What have you got there?"

His garrulousness shocked me. Why was he drunk so early in the day? Why? Where was Mary? Was she visiting someone out of town? I figured he was this drunk so early in the day because Mary was not around to tell him to knock it off and put the whiskey bottle back in the cupboard. Burt opened the front door, and I handed him the model of The Santa Maria. Immediately, with a looking of scoffing derision, he asked me,

"What the hell is this for? Are you on the level? You don't think I'm going to take the time to put this pile of junk together, do you, numb head? Do you?"

Full of strong alcohol, Burt's thick boozer's body leaned and weaved. He made a quick, inconsequent step with his left leg to better balance himself. We stared at each other, neither knowing what to say. He did not seem to wish to speak. I looked at his eyes, once bright blue but now pinkish, shot full and flushed with blood, and then at his face which was florid, sweaty, and red. And I thought to myself: *It was an old brandy drinker's face, and one close to an unexpected death or some kind of nasty accident.*

Once, I then remembered across years of time, my uncle Bill, a very smart doctor, had been to our house sometime during the late fifties, and suddenly, he talked to my dad about a patient of his with rosacea. He had said,

"You get it from drinking too much, son. It is a chronic disease affecting the skin of the nose, forehead, and cheeks marked by flushing, followed by red coloration due to dilation of the capillaries with papules and acne-like pustules. Chronic: That means that once you have a condition, it never goes away. Never. You got that?"

I wondered: Did Burt Mahony have a bad case of rosacea? When did he get it? Why won't he be able to stop? Why is drinking sometimes called 'the disease of house painters'?

And then, I walked away from those strange, oblique thoughts, and said to Burt,

"I'll make it for you, sir. I'll make it for you."

Handing me back the model ship, still in the box, Burt said,

"What? Why do you repeat yourself? You been reading the Bible?"

With that, another humble pie question, said to a gabby who would be I, he closed the front door, deporting himself back into his secluded and dark caecum. And that is when, even from outside his house standing near the edge of the geraniums, I heard him yell back at the TV set,

"Damn! Another touchdown. Damn! They must fire that idiot coach since he is not getting the damn job done. Today!"

And it turns out that Burt Mahony was right: Our Irish boys were having a terrible season that year of 1960, and the team would finish the season with a woeful record of 2 wins and 8 losses.

It took me a couple of weeks to assemble 'her', not 'it', since ships, like cars, mountains, and vines are all beautiful, certainly more beautiful than men, and that being so, the word must be made into, characterized forever as a woman. Like 'La barca' for 'The ship'.

It was not an easy job for me to build the ship. The directions were in the smallest print and for that reason hard to read. Sometimes the order was backward. Sometimes, too, after using glue for hours, my little pudgy fingers would get too sticky for me to work on her anymore. And soap, or 'il sapone', as my buddy, Tom, called it, would not make the stickiness go away. Sometimes, as well, the simple tediousness of the project would bear down upon me and make me tired and cranky, or give my neck muscle, the sternocleidomastoid, a bit of a crick or a winkle, and I'd have to stop or go outside to play some ball. I always liked and later recalled the funny names of muscles that my uncle, the smart doctor, would tell me about whenever he visited. On all nice days, which most of ours were, it was a doggone shame or something unfortunate or 'infelice', to stay indoors when one can go outside and get lots of fresh air that came from above the ocean not far away into the lungs.

Over that summer and fall, Dad at first had not realized how many windows, seven, sette, it was that we had broken. But once he did there was hell to pay. So, one night, a Friday, as I was still working on the ship, Dad got in a real lather, or all steamed up about it. At the dinner table, roiled, annoyed beyond the normal, he said,

"I have been thinking. Do you and your fellow dingdongs know that Mr. Burton Mahoney proudly served in the military for both World War I and World War II? He was born in 1900, just like your Uncle Francis. Did you know that fact, rapscallion? And, he was in the United States Navy, just like your dad, and that is doubtless how and why he picked up some strange lingo, probably in distant and exotic ports of call. Son, can you imagine what he has seen? The depravities and bloodshed? Do you think he put his Irish paddy whacker mick ass on the line for our blessed country all those years so that he would come back home to where you would, without shame or modesty or apology of any kind, break so darn many of his windows? What exactly has he done to harm you? What?"

So, I told Dad that I was building the ship for Burt, doing a good job and taking my bosun's time, trying to make her as best I could. Dad asked,

"Did you ever tell him you were sorry, son? Did you? Or have you remained obdurately unthinking and arrogant?"

I bowed my small, yeoman's head in a child's unvarnished shame and said,

"No. But I will. I will when I finish it, her, which will be tomorrow. Domani. Tomorrow. And sir, we no longer play baseball in the street."

So, then it was, that she, The Santa Maria, was finished, done. Strongly colored, dressed up in the gayest of colors, flags, festooned with flags, what the Italians call 'Le bandiere', of the widest range, signifying rank and station and country of origin: Spain. It is odd Italy had not wanted him even though he was born a Genovese. All the guns on the ship were mounted and readied for firing. All the ropes were arranged as they would be prepared for action, if the ship were at sea. And all the sails must be fully opened, with the largest of billows, to catch all the gusting trade winds. She must be made fully ready as if she truly were at sea, at sea, or 'al mare'.

Thus, I was then ready to take her back, completed, to Burt. Would he be mad? Would he yell at me? Would he smile at me and show me one more time his yellowed or tan teeth? Still, I did not wish to be yelled at, nor to drop it, her, as I set out across the street, holding, cradling her, my baby ship, closely in both my hands.

Again, scared, I knocked on their front door. Immediately, I thanked God that Mary answered the door; but maybe I should not say that since it turned out that Burt was in a good mood as well, the finest fettle. In a loud seaman's voice, he bellowed, hollered, even though I stood close to him,

"How are you, boy? Well, I hope. Is everything ship-shape today? Tidy? What you got there, son?"

Tentatively, gingerly, I passed with both hands Santa Maria over to Burt. He took her and smiled, studying the ship. He held her up and turned her this way and that, inspecting the forecastle, the hull, the crow's nest, the bridge. He saw all the different flags and billowing sails. He even tested the rigging for proper tautness. Finally, he said,

"Well, you have done a fine job here, young man. Thank you. Indeed, I will enjoy looking at her for many years since, as you know, I am a long way from casting my last anchor. Thank you again, sonny."

While he had been examining The Santa Maria, I was thinking: This 60-year-old man had been in two wars. What slaughter he must have seen, what bedlam, what atrocities, what mayhem! And he had landed here at this small house so that I could break seven of his windowpanes, 'sette lastre'. At last, guilt's incipiency finally within me, and, for a few moments, I came close to tears.

While he studied the ship, I looked at his face and then his eyes. Today, they were clear. They were a small window for me to see how hard his life had been. His face was etched with lines from squinting into the Pacific sun. And his bright blue eyes, the color of freedom, mirrored his soul: A bit disconsolate, disgruntled, and wistful. Had a child of theirs died unexpectedly, as but a baby, and yet, they did not wish to speak of it, that unexpected and sudden death? I tried to remember the glimpse or edge of that sad rumor that I had heard once, fleetingly, from my mom. Striding quickly, Mary entered the small living room, and she said to me, in a loud, clear voice,

"What have we here? How beautiful. Would you care for some cake, young man, or maybe a cold glass of milk?"

Older women of that era, one now long gone, usually asked that question of the neighborhoods' children at least once a week. I replied,

"No. Thank you, Mrs. Mahoney."

"Please call me Mary. How about those M&M boys? And the Yankees! For sure the best team in baseball will make the series, but will they win it? I ask you! Sometimes the unexpected happens!"

That fine day they, both Burt and Mary were both on a talker's path, fulfilling their innate Irish destiny to talk a lot, to harangue, to divert, or flap the gums. Yet, I felt the need to depart, to escape this older world to which I did not belong.

However, I needed to look at Burt once again, and more closely. I studied him as a doctor would his patient, someone whose disease had not yet been properly foretold by tests or blood or pus or swellings. I thought: *How did he ever muster such strength?* True: His company was not easy. He was a 'No bullshit' kind of guy, the kind of man our country used to produce back then in spades. How could I, a little kid, ever know him? He was a painter and one to often paint the town red, a Mick, a Paddy whacker, a sailor in two wars, a survivor of the depression, a husband, a father; and what was I? A kid who knows nothing, and one who had broken his windows. Lieutenant Colonel James Doolittle did much (as my dad used to say: He Went Over the Hump, Over the Hump to China), and so had Burt Mahony. Both men were heroes. Mesmerized by these thoughts, I glanced at him for the last, tangled time and thought of him: *Yes, his life had been hard, hard, and that is why, how, he was sometimes a little hard-boiled, hand-bitten, and rough around the edges.* Every dingbat like me, every dipshit schmo that walks in his door, he gives a feisty grilling to, and why not engage in such aggressive repartee? Why not? No. His company was not easy. Yet, I had stayed too long, so lost in thought, as one does. I shuffled my feet. Then I cleared my throat with a small cough, and said to both Mary and Burt,

"I am very sorry for breaking your windows. It was foolish and thoughtless of me to do it. I apologize to both of you sincerely. From now on, we shall play baseball at the park. It will not happen again."

Embarrassed and not wanting to look either of them in the eye, I shuffled out. As I left, both were heard to say,

"Don't worry, son. Don't worry. All is forgiven. All is forgotten."

And so, I departed. As I walked past the plot of geraniums, I looked over my shoulder at the window, studying it carefully, and for the first time, I counted the number of windowpanes: There were sixty-four.

And today I think: Instead of breaking windows, had I not committed another crime? Did I not steal, like Mercury, this small story from the past? Did I not steal it from the past, from someone on the ropes, maybe close to death, and race it forward, twisting it always to my best advantage, putting myself always in the best possible light? Light: That charge of illusion or the real thing? I remember from my dad the German word, 'Urlicht', for 'primal light'. Every schmo that walks through here thinks he is an Einstein. Again, I am not. Therefore, dingus, oldster, and groom: On whom should one rely? On whom?

In any case, now, because this tiny tale is written, Burt lives on. Litera scripta manet: The written word endures. In fact, Burt is here, smiling, sitting here next to me, since by this time we have both passed to the next life. Many years have gone by, but Burt is still older than I, and I know that I shall not catch up to him ever. In my eyes, we are telling each other only the raciest, the dandiest, and the silliest of stories. We take turns, and first he talks to me, telling a good one, and then I start in. He is much better with all the words and the funny telling of them than I am, which is not at all surprising since he has had considerably more practice. We are both eager for any tale of mirth, and we are always on the edge of a rapturous guffaw or rankest counter. Who can tell a joke the best? He knows, more than I do, that practice makes perfect. Always, his kind and dancing bright blue eyes say to me now,

"Get ready for a war. Prepare for the contest. Sir, friend: Gird yourself for battle. The situation is desperate, drastic, dire, but not serious, boy, do you hear me? Not serious at all. That is the way all proper Irishmen think, do you hear me? Now: Begin! I shall say it again: Begin! Move it! Begin!"

Over fifty years later my son and I returned to precisely the same neighborhood, the same scene, yet some things had changed. Again examining the ornate brass handle of our front door, the one with the scalloped edges and considerable deep pitting due to the ocean's closeness, I looked across the street to see the bright pink Mahony house; however, it was gone, entirely gone. In the intervening years, it had been razed and replaced with a three-story glass and concrete monstrosity. Of course, it had. The new owners did not want the original house owned by Burt and Mary Mahony, but only the land upon which it rested, since, after all, the plot of land remains only a quick three blocks from the ocean. Thus, today, the only trace left, the only true proof that Burt and Mary Mahony had once lived there is via memory: Their story is fixed and immutable in our minds. By the way, of course, that large window with sixty-four windowpanes of glass is gone and so is that carefully tended plot of geraniums which was once just to the west of the window, at that brief time making it that much closer to the sea.

The beatniks down on the strand, living right next to the surf, so close that they could have heard the constant roar of the ocean as they drifted off to humble sleep, those old, tan, and wrinkly guys who never worked and who seemed to spend all their time grilling chicken, drinking cheap red wine, smoking funny-smelling marijuana cigarettes, and smiling at their wives or girlfriends—they made a kid like me wonder: Had they too, like Burt, fought in the war against the Japanese or the Germans? Did they battle against the Italians at Anzio or Montecassino? These beatniks lived in the smallest of houses called bungalows, which forever remains a funny word out of the mainstream. If it were a decent day, they spent much time outside, shirtless and bearded, and since their women, occasionally topless, would join them, my dad, always alert and keen, acting like one of Lieutenant Colonel George Custer's vigilant scouts, stopped to chat, to discuss the always changing weather. As he did so, inevitably, Dad would say to me confidentially,

"Free view,"

and then he would wink at me, man to man. And that is when my mom, standing right there with us, would scowl and say more than once,

"I never."

But all of that took place many years ago. Nearly all the tiny and cramped bungalows, full of memories, salt, sand fleas and chiggers, drywood termites, and the smell of iodine and seaweed taken from the sea, have been razed for houses bigger, much bigger. After the land skyrocketed in value, the rent for the beatniks predictably followed suit, climbing to stratospheric levels, and soon the beatniks and their women could not afford to live their anymore, so, all I can figure is that they must have moved down the road to someplace else.

An Accident Unforeseen

It was at least seven miles on my ten-speed bicycle from our house in the center of the valley to the Parker Ranch on its northwest edge, and all the time I was heading steadily uphill, pedaling past faded, leaning trailers, tractor repair shops, broken down and disabled trucks, and forty yards of signs advertising 'Ojala: The resort from the Chumash'. My mother had told me earlier that day that Ojala was a Spanish word meaning 'A strong desire for something to come to pass'. And, as soon as I reached the last of the signs, as if by singular or whimsical chance, a small pebbled road or uneven lane led off the smooth tarmac of the highway to the sky-high ranch where I worked with the citrus trees, mostly navel and Valencia oranges, with some Meyer lemons thrown in for good measure. The trees were planted tightly together there on the thirty-odd acres of that east-facing mesa, one situated well above the Ventura River far below. The Army Corps of Engineers had dammed the small river back in 1948 when concrete was cheaper than bread and thought by some to be more useful. However, the slow lights or bright bulbs who designed it had not counted on the friable soil under the river, and how fast, when touched by water, especially running water during the rainy season, the moving soil would build and mound or turn to silt. So, it was a distinct surprise to many of them when just a few years later, before the concrete had had time to begin to cure itself and to become as strong as it would ever be, the area behind the dam nearly filled with silt. Therefore, the lake behind it held only a small percentage of the water it was meant to hold, and, under the water, held back by the dam which by now had developed the smallest crack or cleft, sat tons and tons, cubic yards and cubic yards, of mud, black and alluvial mud.

But, as any boy would, I thought of none of these monstrous and moneyed issues as I pedaled my trusty ten-speed bike always going uphill to work. I was only glad to have a job, that of a ranchman's assistant. I irrigated the trees, planted new ones, scouted for gophers, sprayed diesel fuel against the weeds (especially mare's tail and field bindweed), and laid out additional blocks for new plantings should my boss one day come up to me to say that he had the money, which he also called 'The scratch' or 'The green'.

Mr. Parker, he wasn't such a bad guy. He did not try to be bad, but again, nor did he try very hard to be good. He was comfortably in the middle, or, at least, so I sometimes thought. The truth is, I rarely saw him, and I only thought about him when he was around. So, most of the time, I thought about the job at hand, or, it must now be admitted, many other things, like baseball, or certain nameless and always drifting girls—those pretty and nameless female forms that lurked with what I felt was small, mocking derision at the edge of my young teenager's brain.

Mr. Parker was having an affair, or so he told me when I first started. He said,

"I don't want to hear any frikkin' gossiping, do you hear me, whelp? I'm carrying on with a dilly gal at the bank, but I'm not telling you her name, understand? This is on a need-to-know basis, dingus. You got a problem with that, my new customer?"

I said to my new boss,

"No way, sir. That's your business, and not mine. I'll keep my big trap shut, I promise you. My dad says I should have been a damn spy."

"Good. Good. Tell your dad he may be right. Now listen to me. Here is a bunch of stuff I want you to get done, before I get back. Parker is going to park it. That's a joke, buddy. After all, it's noon and the sky is high."

And then he'd ramble on in this crazy, hard-to-follow Oakie twang of his with a long list of things to get done, so many things that always I'd only be able to get half, or maybe even less, accomplished. I got it: He didn't want me standing around, whistling dixie, engaging in pipe dreams, cleaning tools, sorting rakes, or wasting time in any way. Parker was tight-fisted with money, but even though I was only fourteen, I had seen tightwads who were worse about money. And, as he left that day, leaving in one of his many restored pick-ups, in a surprising action that I could not have foretold, Parker leaned out the side window of his truck and said to me, as if I were someone important whom he had known for a long time,

"It was an accident. The whole thing was a flipping accident. I didn't mean to leave my wife. No sir. She was a good gal. Dependable and decent. I got to go."

And then he sped off, his old, and dented Chevy truck making a tall plume of sandy or tan dust which rose up high into the windless, cloudless sky, with his truck spraying small riverbed stones, pebbles, and rocks all over the place, his tires making churning, squealing noises all the way up the walls of the canyon from which distant place they would return to me reverberating, downward, toward my ears, my still tender ears.

Weeks earlier, just after I first started working on the Parker Ranch, one of my high school buddies from town had told me that Mr. Parker had been quite the football star ten years earlier. Stocky, swarthy, and through a kind predisposition, one directed by a kindly God, possessive of an eternally white set of gleaming teeth, nearly too big for his smaller mouth, Mr. Parker, Larry by first name, had been the star halfback on the high school football team, the one that back in the day nearly went to the state finals. One game near the end of the season (and no one neither alleged, nor intimated that it had been planned), Larry was hurt badly on a play. He had been caught in one of those enormous piles of boys all heaped willy-nilly on top of each other that occurs at the ends of many plays; but, on this one, while his left leg was pinched between two other unowned limbs, shockingly it had been stepped on by one of his own teammates, Paul Magro, who weighed almost 300 pounds. The crisp snap of the longer lower leg bone, the tibia (from the Latin word for pipe), could be heard by the hundreds of spectators clearly as a shepherd's whistle, the awful telltale sound traveling swiftly from the place of the injury on the field up into the stands. And so ended in an instant Larry's football career.

It was then no surprise that 'LP', as he sometimes called himself, got into citrus farming. The ranch on the east-facing high mesa had been in his family for many decades. Farming had been in his blood. In his teenage years, Larry had not been much of a student, since, as he often said,

"There are way too many fat jerkoffs telling me what to do all the time. What ever happened to freedom?"

And, after his parents both passed away early, his dad worn out from sheer fatigue and his mom from some sort of runaway female cancer, Larry, an only child, inherited the farm, whether he wanted the gorgeous and prestigious piece of ground or not.

I remembered the day around a month ago when I first asked him for work. He had been gruff, stern, and frankly, an ass. And, why not? He said, challenging me,

"Buddy, you want to work or just screw around? I have to tell you that I'm darn leery of you youngsters. I don't want any half-assed lazers or layabouts working on the Parker Ranch. Understood? What's your choice?"

I responded quickly to my new boss,

"First, I'll have to prove to you, by my actions, that I'm not a slacker or shirker."

And that's how it all started.

Thankfully, like I said before, most of the time he left me alone. One day, I heard him operating the backhoe at the far end of the ranch, just below Mount Jameson whose big-nosed profile makes that mountain look like an angry Indian's face. I cannot blame them for being angry. This was near the eroded barranca that slopes steeply down to a trickling creek. Sometimes there I'd catch a glimpse of teenagers skinny dipping, girls with long curly hair and no modesty, and skinny guys with no muscles. But, on this day, I had headed that way to change over an irrigation set, and suddenly, Mr. Parker came around a corner of the orchard, driving the backhoe, smiling a crazy, hilting, manic smile since in the front-end loader, plopped there awkwardly and flopping around, was a horse, a dead horse. I guess he was getting ready to bury it. But he sat there on the tractor with the biggest grin on his face, like some nutty guy out of a Grade B horror movie from the forties who had either just got out of the insane asylum or just whacked someone at the end of a bar fight.

However, most of the time he was gone, off the ranch, and I was happy about that, since he was probably either sweeping the floor with his dilly girl from the bank or playing cards, poker. One of my buddies, Charlie O'Halloran, told me that Larry was one of the best poker players in town, no, in all of Ventura County. A group of guys would get together whenever they did not feel like working, which was often, citrus ranchers like Larry mostly, usually at the Ram Lodge down the highway, or, sometimes, The Wagon Train bar downtown, and they would play 'Pokerino', as he liked to call it, for hours and hours, intentionally killing the whole afternoon. All of that didn't bother me one little bit since his absence meant that he would not be around to pester me, to scold or rail at me, or to hound, looking over my shoulder like some sort of pest.

Not long after that, Charlie told me (he was one of those guys whose ear was always close to the ground, whose nose is constantly near somebody's tail) that there had recently been a bad shootout outside the Ram Lodge: A card game had gone wrong, where one rube hayseed had accused another of the usual, which would be cheating, and a pistol had been discharged.

Nobody got hurt; but even an in-the-cups Goober knows that pistols never fire themselves. Charlie said (and I am wondering: How the heck did he know all this?) that the gun had been fired, only once, by a Mexican guy, some young, hot-headed stranger from Durango, who it was said, whispered, had once spent some time in prison, the hoosegow, the joint, or the clink. I was sure Larry had been there that day playing 'Pokerino' and I thought how Larry, my boss, could easily have been shot, once, right into the heart, that is, if the loco guy from Durango had been at all accurate or precise. I don't think Larry ever cheated at cards, so maybe the Mexican was steamed up, sozzled, mostly on too much beer or cheap whiskey, since he had imagined that his wife had left him or wanted to, so that he had no choice but to get fast boozed up and therefore crazy, to become a bottle-man intent on making a ruckus, to eventually be blotto, liquored-up, lubricated, or, or as he himself might have said if his lips could move or had worked well enough to say these three familiar words,

"Muy borracho, bendajo!"

When next I saw Larry, he seemed particularly pissed off, that is, more than his normal grouchy self, so I was of absolutely no mind to ask him about the shooting for two reasons: The first is I did not want to give him a chance to bark at me, to bark like a crazy or rabid or deranged dog might; and secondly, I did not want to hear him vent his spleen against all Mexicans. Even though I had not worked on Parker's Ranch for very long, barely one month, already I knew that he hated them, whom he sometimes called 'lazy sombreros' or 'greasy beaners', with an unguarded and idiotic racist's passion, saying,

"They're taking our jobs away, one by one, the bastards, and we let them do it because we're lazy and stupid. Kid, it is that simple. It is no accident that by their much higher birth rate, they're simply, day by day, taking over our country. Those soldiers are working without a helmet. These darn Mexicans breed like crazy, like rabbits. They crank our kids like they're splitting and stacking oak cordwood."

I had heard that same stupid speech, full of venom and cant, so many times before, and I did not want, if possible, to hear it again. Sometimes, as my dad often said, "Silence is golden." So, I often enjoyed those quick moments of the golden.

Some time passed. The days began to shorten as they always do that time of year. It may have been early August, but I cannot be sure. I only could know or recognize, and therefore later remember the winds, harsh, drying, and fiercely blustery winds that would barrel down the steeper canyons from the spreading regions of the Sespe Wilderness far to the northeast. I knew that August would bring with it like heavy luggage or too much salt in food, these Santa Ana winds which quickly would dry out, desiccate, everything that they touched. Then, inevitably, as predictable as an old and feeble count who at night cannot find his way from the bathroom back to bed, forest fires would erupt, dozens of them, scorching thousands of acres in a flash, in an instant. And beyond that, in this August month of the Santa Ana winds, occasionally, for no reason at all, the most random of human violence would spark, resulting in senseless and chaotic mayhem or tragedy. Police chiefs in the area, Charlie would tell me, were always happy when August was done, over with, because that meant that people, most of them anyway, could return to normal and relearn how to behave like proper human beings one more time.

That day, in what must have been stern August, early in the dew of morning, I had pedaled seven miles northwest. Not only was I, at only 14, too young to drive, but I also thought and had long believed that gasoline was a huge waste of money. Stupid. Just another snow job or con. What is wrong with a bike? People keep pumping expensive gasoline into 4,000-pound cars and then act surprised when they end up broke. Dumb, like feeding the monkey bananas, with no end to the feeding.

Poverty is no accident, or so I then thought. Besides, I thought, *I like to pedal: It was good for my legs and always made them feel like two, carefully compressed springs.*

That day I had pedaled hard and northwest out of the valley proper toward the impassable Sespe Wilderness, past orange and lemon grooves starting to become heavily laden with fruit, past the garages and shops filled with derelict tractors and trucks, past Mrs. Zimmer's house where sometimes, usually in the afternoon after work when I was easily pedaling southeast down the river valley, if I spied sharply enough, at just the right second, instant, at the perfect spot on the road's corner, I would see her in her backyard, her tanned and curvy body held graciously within her bathing suit: Chartreuse, it was, one day that cannot be forgotten, with her voluptuous body reclining on the natural teak chaise-lounge, like some famous and rich Hollywood has-been movie star, of which the valley was becoming full, laden. But enough of that quick, tantalizing vision, I quickly decided, since, thinking with a teenager's quick brain: What firm joy does it give, and what bigger harm does it engender?

Finally, I pedaled past the Matilija Hot Springs where the emergent hippies would smoke their treasured weed as if it were something rare and holy and sacred. They would then retreat to the shallow pools and rocky recesses where they gathered in some sort of ersatz and phony communion. There, two or more of them might cavort, unseen by any prying eyes, including mine, since I had to go to work, to keep the hungry wolf away from the door and his tongue in his mouth. It still slays me how, nine months later, some on the distaff side of things and their skinny, no-muscle temp boys, with arms like breadsticks or grissini, would act surprised and bewildered when she of the hairy armpits would pop out a baby. What were they thinking? They must think it cool to play hide the salami without wearing a helmet. These dumb heads act most astonished and surprised when a kid arrives. Don't these numb nuts know how one gets a bun in the oven or a plane in the hanger?

Do they think it is through the considerate action of a stork that children are made? It can take as little time as three minutes to make a girl preggers, knocked up, with child, but these hippies lurking in the shadow of pools along the creek must not have ever had these dove thoughts. Unplanned pregnancy? A contradiction in terms! What do these dims, and getting dimmer longhairs think is going to happen? That their toenails are abruptly going to grow faster when they do the dirty? That they were suddenly be able to hit a sharp breaking curve? Fiddlesticks. Air heads. Dummies. More and more, I was getting fed up with their endless cant and dross.

Maybe they just do not give a darn or fiddle one way or the bother, and just like the fleeting moment's passing pleasure.

By this time, having passed the final Ojala sign, I had reached the narrow, curving, and rutted lane that led from the highway down to the rocky creek bed. A narrow wooden bridge spanned the creek, and over the years, it had gotten slippery, glazed slick by all the trucks carrying sweet oranges busting over it all these years, which meant that I had to be careful, extra careful, as I approached it. Then, just after crossing the creek, I would sometimes smell there the rankest smell of the creek's bushes, scrubs, and cattails, it varying some depending on the season. A kind of vegetative perfumed smell always lingered there next to the small river as a type of balm or incense, and it always made me smile. Often the aroma next to the trickling Ventura River would remind me of the pungent aroma of sausage casing.

Soon, I left that weedy creek bed fragrance and had to pedal harder up the steep incline to the ranch. At one corner, I had to stand up on the bike, so steep was the grade and if I didn't, I would keel over sideways. Suddenly, unforeseen, the road had gotten very sharply uphill while I was heading west, always heading west, and I could feel the growing strength of the morning sun positioned in the early morning sky far to the east upon my back and neck. The morning fog had by now mostly lifted. I could feel my little boy's beating heart racing ever faster in my small, boney chest.

Soon, following the road rutted by thousands of tires passing, since it was never repaired, never regraded, never re-graveled, I passed Larry's simple farmhouse, which needed a new coat of paint like most of them did out here in the country. Only on the north side of the house, the side that faced upriver, toward the yawning expanse of the Sespe, could a fellow paying half-attention see the house's original color, that is, before it had faded from the relentless onslaught of the sun. There it was a Prussian blue, a combination of grey and blue, close enough to the blue of the British Air Force uniform, that of the R.A.F. With the pulses of the sun, the paint on the house had lightened considerably, especially on the exposed southern and western side of the simple structure. There, in blotchy spots, it seemed more like a Battleship grey, or the color of the hull of a ship.

By this time, breathing hard and starting to sweat, I had reached the mesa's apex. If I had possessed eyes in the back of my head, I could have seen directly behind me and high up in the sky, the mountainous ridge of the surprising Topa Topa, the clefts and verdant folds of the other upper valleys, the rocky beginnings of San Antonio Creek far to the east, that is, before she gathered to herself all the waters that led her down to the sea just north of Ventura seventeen miles away. As it was, pedaling still but more easily now on the near flatness of the mesa, a table of land only slightly inclined, by looking straight ahead, west, I could again see the outline of Jameson Peak (Was it really like the profile of an Indian warrior, a fierce Chumash and I already knew why he was angry.) And, beyond the mountain, though I could not see them, I knew that other smaller purple and sage-covered mountains encircled the city of Santa Barbara close to the sea. Somewhere down the backside of Jameson is the county line, but who gives a darn? Elmer and nobody else but a bunch of long-haired, head-in-the-clouds dope smokers go up into that rough country anymore.

Eventually, I reached the ranch's large barn, which was probably twice as big as Larry's farmhouse. It was filled with all the necessary and unnecessary things that occupy any of these old and disused barns: Worthless worn tires, broken tractor parts, dead batteries, tangles of ropes and rusty chains, cracked clevises, weed sprayers with pulsating pumps about to pack it in, all manner of hard tools illogically arranged, chain saws that won't start and whose chains need sharpening, dusty hand drills with bent bits, and electric saws, most with dull, warped blades and dangerously frayed electrical cords just at that elbowed point where they come out of the base of the machines. Also arrayed about the barn were some scattered signs of human life: A leftover bologna sandwich left to dry and curve, a can of Coke still with an inch of soda at the can's bottom, a half-eaten apple, fully browned now, forgotten and at rest upon the grimy, disordered workbench.

Earlier, Larry had told me, no, rather, he barked,

"Kid, listen. I want you to prune the orchard. It will take the rest of the summer. Get going! Here are the loppers you'll need. Get your fingers out of your nose, doofus. Now, go! Go!"

He had delivered this typical speech to me the night before. He had told me he wouldn't be around today. I suspected that he had spent the night at his bank gal's place (Once, he had leered to me, "I got to make a deposit; no, two!"), and by now, still early, he was probably cuddling up next to her, smelling deeply into her full female body's curves, coaxing the retreat of his hangover that had arrived placidly, stealthily, and, now, as before, with near every new sun, trying to make it go away. However, I did not want to think of that anymore because to think of my jerk-off boss in bed with some lady, someone whose name I never learned, that is a paltry thought that does me no good at all no matter how short or long I hold it close. I had long ago promised myself to harbor only pleasant or charitable thoughts which are productive and helpful, or also, those few rare ones which are more than that.

And so, with that damper, I set off, grabbing Larry's old loppers, probably also in need of a sharpening, and his extension ladder, a new aluminum one with a nylon rope attached to it, the kind that you pull down to make it get longer. The lopper was one of the heavy, genuine ones still made by Corona and the serious handle which was one of the good ones made of real hickory, so that you couldn't break it if you tried. The blades were nearly 3 inches long, leading to a point, and though, since the hand tool was old, they weren't all that sharp, I reckoned that they were still sharp enough to get the job done.

Right away I could sense that it was going to be a hot mother today. Maybe because the Santa Ana winds were coming, the fog had lifted earlier than normal. No clouds or mist were in the sky. It, she, was blue, the color of a robin's egg, the brightest blue that there is, and no doubt a harbinger of a much deeper heat for the afternoon. I knew in advance that the day would soon be offering up the sort of sultry heat where it is almost hard to breathe, and it is darn easy for anyone to feel light-headed and a bit dizzy, unsteady on one's feet. I was glad that Larry had left a 5-gallon metal water jug which I could fill from the water bib at the edge of the barn; plus, if I wanted to, I could pinch some ice cubes out of the groaning refrigerator where he kept his stash of Acme beer, it made in downtown Los Angeles close by the river of the same name.

I started out on the Valencia orange trees closest to the barn, working on one side only. I was giving them 'A haircut' only on the side facing the creek, pruning off roughly a foot of vegetation, of the waxy, dark green leaves. I tried not to cut off any of the fruit, any of the nearly ripe Valencia oranges since I could see that old Larry had a pretty good crop here, and, as the ranchman's assistant, I wanted to guard it for him, to keep and retain it all. Holding the old, out-of-tune loppers in my right hand and grasping the ladder with my left, that morning I pruned and climbed, trimmed and descended, tens, hundreds of times. Occasionally, a flock of geese would come by to peck at my pants, and to pee and poo, but I threw rocks toward them, not to hurt them, but to startle, to make them and their awfully loud, bleating noises go away.

This was the kind of job where a person had plenty of time to think. I reflected that Larry had, more and more, left the ranch. He was hardly ever here! He was either 'Sawing off a piece' or playing 'Pokerino' with the gaggle of farming geezers at the Ram Lodge. He never drank anything besides cola when he was playing cards with the boys, because, as he once told me, to do so,

"Would make my blessed judgment go all nutsy."

Thinking it was probably odds-on better to leave the lopper on the ladder's top rung, both to save time and be safer, two-handedly climbing the ladder, I thought how Larry leaving the ranch so much of the time left it open for abuse, and growing neglect. Moving the ladder to the next tree, I wondered if, down the road, because of his growing preoccupation with cards and nookie, not necessarily in that ignoble order, that maybe, if he were not more careful and judicious, he'd lose it in foreclosure to some git airhead, maybe some ineffectual pinstriped, empty suit at the bank. And, just then, suddenly, out of the blue and as quickly as anything can ever happen, I felt the sharpest and deepest sting at the top of my right shoulder.

Yes, on the Erie, the lopper had fallen from the top rung of the ladder at the rate of 32 feet per second per second from a height of more than 10 feet. The blades, rusted, open, and separated, had traveled first, ahead of the handles, because they were the heaviest. One of them, nearly three inches long and banana-curved to a point, whilst I was looking forward not knowing what was about to happen next, struck the fleshy muscular part of my right shoulder, in particular, the deltoid's outer rounded expansion, and embedded itself deeply there. This was an accident unforeseen, one of many surprises that a full life offers. The pain was tolerable, but the bloody mess a distraction. With my free left hand, I reached across my chest, with much blood already gathering there, dislodged the lopper, and threw it viciously to the earth. Then, for the fleetest of seconds, in much less time than it took my man Mickey in his prime to reach first base (in 1951 before he hurt his knee, the same year I was born, it took only 3.1 seconds for Oklahoma's Commerce Comet to cover that 90 feet), I spied sharply deep into the wound and saw there, just for a tick, the whitest of bone, my humerus, just beyond or below the scapula and clavicle. Such a brief sighting made me think of bone China or milk or vanilla ice cream, which would be my favorite. The wound still didn't hurt much, but I was worried about blood loss since if anyone loses much more than half of the 10 pints allocated by a benevolent God to him, then he is for sure a goner, a stiff, or lights out, and then pretty soon, rigor mortis will set in, so I took off my grimy tee shirt, the one advertising the Joliet Convicts Baseball Club of Illinois, a honky-tonk river town that I had never seen, and pressed it hard and tight against the wound. Fibrin, to stanch the Amazon flow of blood out of my body, I wondered: *When would it begin to work its coagulating magic?*

I began to skip or stumble toward the farmhouse. I needed help and had to call home. I could not ride my bike to the hospital bleeding like a stuck pig, like some animal shot at close range two or three times by a 12 gauge. I was glad the uneven gravel road was downhill. I tripped often on rocks, ruts, roots, and the natural unevenness of the ground. Finally, breathing hard, the tee shirt by this time nearly all crimson or vermillion with blood, I walked into Larry's small ranch house. (I am today still thankful that Larry had not locked it, so trusting people were back then that little mischief would occur.) There, hanging on the wall, as in thousands of farmhouses everywhere, was the phone. I dialed. Grandma answered, she of proud Norwegian stock and nearly 77 years, 6 feet in height, long-limbed and fleshy, strong like a man but feminine in her face and figure, pushing 200 pounds if not a stone more, the patient preparer of thousands of meals, cakes, cinnamon rolls, and pies, and she was asking me,

"Who is this? Who? Is that Tommy?"

I answered,

"No. It's me, Grandma. Nicky. Where's Mom?"

"Do you mean my daughter, young man?"

"The one and the same, Grandma. Your daughter, Florence, is also my mom."

"I haven't seen her since this morning, son. So, do you want me to look?"

I said,

"No," and hung up. Quickly, I thought I should have to solve this riddle, my new conundrum, by other means, different tactics.

And this is where rare Irish luck came in the front door and sat down. Old Larry had a neat, sterling, and small collection of old pickup trucks: Fords, Dodges, Chevys, Studebakers, you name it, and he always left the key in the ignition, which was a good thing, otherwise, sure as anything, a pale horse might have trotted by. I chose a dark green, cherried-out Stude (Was it a 1948? Maybe 1949? Today, who can precisely pinpoint the exact year of manufacture?), turned the ignition key a bit to the right, and, happy days, as God is my benign witness, the old truck sprang to life. Plus, she possessed a half a tank of gas which was most fortunate. The truck was, of course, a stick, and, since I did not want to use my right arm to shift, I had to reach across my body and shift, awkwardly, with my left arm. The bloody tee-shirt sat on top of my shoulder, and drops of blood ran down onto the seat, down my right leg, pooling and puddling there beneath the pedals. I drove slowly down the bumpy farm lane, and slowed down even more as I neared the slippery, skiddy, glazed-over wooden bridge which traversed the river. Because of the pooled and puddled blood near the pedals, in a flash they had become slippery as well. Once, after crossing the bridge and heading up the steep hill that led back to the highway, I killed the motor because I had the Stude in 2nd gear when I should have had it in 1st. After all, I was only 14 and still learning how to drive. Eventually, fishing far to the forward I found the granny-low gear and, giving the truck a bit more throttle, I motored up the steep gravel hill that led to the pavement. Finally, I reached the highway where the road was smooth and even and where it was much easier to drive, and I thought if the cops stop me because I look too young to drive or I don't have a license, I would stuff them. A nasty argument or niff-naw might ensue. I figured that most cops are stupid blokes, gun nuts, or have a disordered, short-man complex like they say Napoleon did. Some of them are overpaid stooges who like the badge and the fat health-care benefits and the fat pension after they retire. And some of them are slow headed show-offs with not enough brains to add 2 and 2. 'Five' they would slowly say, 'Five'.

Just then, a cop drove by me, fast, heading northwest into the Sespe Wilderness. I had my Dodger hat on, pulled down low and tight unto my head, shielding my young, virgin's face from the policeman's view. Fortunately, in a hurry to burn the county's gasoline and go nowhere (I imagined that maybe he had a new girlfriend farther up the canyon), the copper did not stop or even slow. So, down the highway I went, mostly traveling slightly downhill, heading southeast for the seven miles, driving slowly, at around 45 MPH, not wanting to shift, keeping it in 4th gear all the time until I reached the disorganized and straggly edge of town. Clutching the truck like the expert I wasn't, I down-shifted into 3rd gear. Finally, there, on the left, was the hospital. Right away, I saw the big, red sign: Emergency. Grazing the curb's edge with the old Stude's left-front tire, I entered the parking lot and drove over to the Emergency Entrance. Then the Stude hit another curb, I shut the motor off, swung open the driver's door with my good left arm, and walked into the hospital, where I saw, with more than a little adolescent amusement, the wide eyes of the good-looking, brown, and tan nurses when they saw all the blood. Soon, their wide eyes got wider. They all had such pretty faces, and such fine figures. There was one, a Mexican, who caught my young, leering eye. Would this be a good time, I wondered, to arrange a date? Why not, Priscilla, why not? I knew that right then I had her keen attention and sympathy. Plus, I knew already that it was no good being shy or too cautious. I thought of that key line from the Bible,

"Seek and you will find, knock and the door shall be opened to you."

So, to that first one, the pretty, brown-haired Mexican who came up to me, I said, a bit woozily,

"Why are all nurses so pretty?"

Right away, she with the very white teeth told me to be quiet.

Just then, a youngish doctor came out to look at his stinko, bloody victim, me, now deeply submerged in wallowing shock. He looked at me slowly, steadily, and then said, as any comedian's assistant might,

"Your face. Your face. It is covered with pimples, and acne. We have got to fix your face!"

I told him to quit being such a mean jerk, or a stinking Polly gagger, and to please just fix my shoulder. Regarding my face,

"Leave it alone," I told him.

"Just clean the shoulder wound and close it up, please, doctor."

My folks must have come down later to the hospital to pick me up. I don't remember for sure, since my mind was still not working right. Later that night, the shoulder began to throb with each heartbeat of my little boy's heart. Still later that long night, my dad gave me a few nips of a fine French cognac, Hine. My parents drank Hine,

"Whenever we could afford it," as my mom used to say, and since it was Winston Churchill's favorite. And Jaspers, how the hell she knew that I'll never know, probably just like so many other things about which a young fart like me can then or now only wonder.

Later that night, I did not tell them about how it was a good thing my man, Larry, had left the keys in the ignition of the dark green Stude. At least, I had not been forced to cross that mean bridge on foot, or to hitchhike the seven miles to town. And, jeeps be Jesus, I finally remembered to thank God for all small favors. I figured I would keep that small detail to myself. I had been lucky, most lucky. As it was, I calculated that they did not need to know everything, since some things are better left on the Q.T, or quiet.

It was quite early the next morning, right after I woke up and felt the sharp pain of the sutured wound to the deltoid muscle of my right shoulder that I realized that I was a dumb cluck not to have seen the accident coming. I looked at my right shoulder and I could see that the wound, sutured shut, must have wept and bled some during the night, since the bandage was bright red and slightly moist with blood. After breakfast of scrambled eggs, sourdough toast, and coffee, Mom said to me,

"Let's take a look at the wound to your shoulder, sonny."

Since she was a surgical nurse, she knew exactly what she was doing, and in less time than it takes to say, 'Connecticut River Valley' that is, before I knew what was coming, I was as good as new.

Feeling still a bit woozy from last week's accident unforeseen, as I lay in bed considering both the foolishness of my accident and also the day ahead, I recalled another surprising incident. I remembered the spring day a few years earlier when, standing in the broad schoolyard before the start of the day, I tried to put a Saint Christopher medal cast in two shades of green around Judy Hudson's pretty neck. Even today I can call back my memory of how deeply tan her neck was, even before the start of summer. Yet, in a flash, once again unexpectedly, standing behind the diminutive Judy, I saw Father Michael O'Connor out of the corner of my eye off in the distance. The Irish priest with the strong brogue of County Meath mightily surprised me, since there was a firm rule at our school that we were not allowed to go steady, no matter what grade we were in. But, since I was surprised, nervous, and fumbling, I dropped it. In a goofy panic, I simply let it go! So, down it went, the religious medal sliding all the way down her flat front until it tinkled, clattered, and scattered itself onto the grey asphalt of the schoolyard. Just then, Father O' Connor walked by, came close to us, and instantly understood exactly what had happened. Looking at me directly, he said to me,

"Son, young man, there's your clear and obvious proof that she is far too young. If she had anything at all up front, that would not have happened."

He smiled and nodded and clicked his teeth together and winked at me as he strode manfully past, for, once again, as a young man then only in fourth grade, I had been taken by surprise.

Father John

Our unchecked, unquestioning embracery of technology was challenged early on for me by a conversation that I had long ago with an Augustinian priest. This priest whom I knew as Father John, provided the initial catalyst by asking the simple and obvious question: Are we better off? The occasion for our discussion was a large Fourth of July jamboree up on Sulphur Mountain at the Wilson Ranch, which watched over, like a sentry might have done, the southern edge of the valley. The large ranch was mostly scrub oak ground used for cattle grazing, but a few acres of Haas and Bacon avocados had recently been planted as an experiment, and as a possible hedge against unreliable beef prices. Years before, the gigantic mountain had earned the moniker 'Sulphur' since sometimes if the Levante winds from the east were brisk and focused, nasty air biscuits, aromas of reduced Sulphur compounds, smelling of rotten eggs or a skunk's exudate, would waft up from San Antonio Creek at the bottom of the mountain onto the hillside, there to disturb and rankle all those who lived there, and for today's big party, the hundreds of revelers.

To get an invite to that special and grandiose annual party meant that you were an eager part of the cognoscenti, and far above the massed hoi polloi. Somehow or other I had wang-dangled one. It was a hot ticket, and I am still not sure I qualified, so my getting one may have been a fluke or accident, something surprising, willy-nilly, and entirely unwarranted. And the Wilsons were most generous to the community at large. There were tons of barbequed rib eye steaks served, with hot, cilantro-containing salsa and buckets of pinto beans, garlic bread, and iced pop, and watermelon quartered, and at least one keg of cold lager beer from which I gingerly partook even though, on that date, I was still more than one year shy of the drinking age of twenty-one. So, I lubricated myself some and looked forward to the chance to chat up some girls who might be friendly for a change and return the favor with a smile. It was one of the first times that I mingled in a party crowd without feeling like a geek, a schnorrer or the town's caustic, looney tunes idiot.

That is when I saw Father John from across the room. He eyed me summarily, as if I were an outlaw outside the law, a renegade ruffian, or homeless bandito, surveying me for any traces of past crimes. He then strode toward me as if he were the town's sheriff, someone packing a long barrel Colt Peacemaker .45 caliber pistol.

At the start of our conversation, little did I anticipate how thoroughly he would soon challenge me. I started out by telling Father John, our kindly parish priest who also played pretty good golf with my dad every Monday morning, how much I enjoyed a Hitchcock class I was taking in college. Specifically, I noted what a great director he was since he could engender, so deftly and so sublimely, such a wide range of conflicting emotions in the viewer, which would be each one of us: First you admire a character, then you hate him and wish him dead, and finally you feel sorry for him and want him protected from any harm. Father John said to me,

"Ah. You must understand more fully. Hitch was just doing his job. He was able to control your emotions so well because you had become like mere dough in his hands; that is, you had become so passive. You ought to know in advance who is running the show. Do not ever sail into danger, son."

In those short words and by extension, he had put in place the idea that rampaging technology and the passivity it relies upon had harmed and was continuing to harm crucially both mental and emotional processes.

In the same way, I now grasp those inveterate users of the computer, that is, most of us I should say, are essentially passive. I propose that we are acted upon by it, and by all the huckstering advertisers who say to buy this, or to try this, or to give this a gentle go. This passivity is intentional, part and parcel of how the computer from its first days was designed to work.

Yet, as an important caveat, there will always be that small fraction of users who are not addicted or too steadily entranced, those who will use the computer for legitimate research. These people are directing it and telling it what to do; so, they are acting, not acted upon.

But, for most of us, those who never saw the advertiser's long left arm reach around their shoulders, we are passive users ready to be sold in the most elaborate, new-fangled, and oh-so-modern fashion. In the meantime, absent has been the use of a word which once informed all dialogue, all learning, and all debate: Sensibility, since what I believe about an idea is less important, or seems so, than ever before. Therefore, the fact that any idea can be beamed into my room has become more central than the idea itself. Sensibility, which is a person's response to a debate, has been made entirely insignificant by the sheer magnitude of the computer's economic thrust and the continent spanning digitized power of the computer.

I was right there waiting and watching on the wings when this computer business commenced, and from the very beginning, reflecting my prior steadfast values as 'The Cynic of the Senior Class', I suspected that it was a hoodwink, mirage, or trick. In the parlance of some born in the ghetto, "I was hep to the jive." And today, so many years later, I resent the thousands of advertisements that pop up on my computer, the sly algorithms that tell me what to buy and in what to believe, and especially, how various new, sly, and addicting forms of social media rob teenagers of their precious youth.

Largely due to Father John's prescient warnings, I grasped that from its incipiency, the manufacture of the computer was primarily mercantile. It had everything to do with making money and nothing to do with curing cancer, stopping foolish wars, or improving literacy, despite what we may have been told at the time. As post-industrial countries, we were casting about for something new to sell (since, apparently, we cannot make anything in this country anymore), enervated by the oil scare or made low by whatever else it is that destroys cultures. So, I suppose in a bitter and ironic way it is good that computers came along. Wow, I can purchase candy bars, soap, or a bottle of Tavel rose wine on the net. However, is this progress? I still miss the chaotic jumble of the street, the odd conversation with a stranger, or the chance to see in person what awful color that pub's mansard has been painted.

Perhaps in this new age that is so hard to grasp, it will be only by my purchases that I shall be known or recognized, not by my tender, half-baked thoughts since they are of no interest to the suppliers of these advances nor to anyone else.

Many trust funders now retreat to their tech cocoons to spend their entire day casting about blog sites that contain extreme opinions only. Propagandists have proliferated beyond anyone's wildest dream; further, they have soiled, perhaps irretrievably, our collective political landscape. Discourse, debate, conversation, a sense of community, and the idea that we are all linked up (Thank you, John Donne), all these factors have shrunk in the face of this new thing, the computer. So, was its introduction such a great victory after all? Let us consider for a moment what other good concepts have been vanquished.

Our individuality has been compromised, and we hardly know it. However, can we not comprise our private dreams of less mercantile issues? Can we not make our dreams ourselves, of unsubstantial cloth or not? Can we not, Blaise, think alone and in a quiet room? Can we not forge an awareness, separate and individually ours, that is not so netted to the net? Why can't we stop being told what to think, what to feel, what to buy? All these questions, of course, and more point toward the one main question that Father John alluded to so many years ago: Who runs the show? Why do so few people today express these misgivings, that the internet is primarily about making money and garnering always additional power to itself, and not exchanging information? Why do so few people lament the loss of human contact that this new world of the computer has inspired? Why have so many people retreated to their computers to grow these outlandish political positions, testaments to loneliness and a lack of moderation and temperance? Who cannot say that the huge cultural schism that we see all around us today was not created in large measure by the monolithic computer, that thing that spawns errant and outlandish ideas out of contact with reality and normal simple human discourse? Still, I often wonder if I am the only one thinking such heretical thoughts that run against the mainstream.

When I was just ten years old, lucky to be living at the beach, I used to swim in the ocean as often as possible. As soon as my little growing bones could stand it, I would submerge myself in the water, chasing away the goosebumps that had formed with quick and constant action, movement. I loved to feel buoyed by the waves, to look for approaching swells, to swim until I was exhausted. I longed then, to return to the seaside to warm myself and to scout keenly for comely and smiling girls. Such were my natural pursuits for many years, and they were ones well-spent. I became slowly but steadily addicted to body surfing, that practiced art of forming my body roughly into the streamlined shape of a log so that I might steadily traverse down the crashing front of a wave. I could feel its mounding and gathering force thrust me toward the shore. Moreover, I did not want to incline myself at too sharp an angle toward the ocean's floor under the wave since to do so might endanger my shoulder or collarbone or, heaven help me, the fragile spinal cord within my neck. Over the years, I became quite skillful at this sport of body surfing, but never good enough. Eventually, we moved away from the sea, and then, as a new landlubber, my acute water-borne skills rapidly declined though want of use.

The point of this small digression is to ask a rhetorical question: Which addiction is healthier? To practice body surfing in the chilly waters of the ocean, or to surf the net? Perhaps most readers may think that body surfing will bring with it greater vigor and, as Cristofaro Columbo once attested, greater hope since it takes place in the sea. You could make the same argument for long-distance bicyclists, those that fish ardently for brown trout, or those that hike the long high ridgeback of Gros Ventre, also known as The Big Belly, in western Wyoming, which rises above the alluvial flats of the Snake River just northeast of Jackson's Hole.

Too, something about reading, to which Father John referred, ought to be mentioned: To do it well, one must do it slowly, allowing the mind to carefully pour over and digest the gist of the author's aim. It is, pointedly, not a visual event. Rather, it is seeing the words on the page and then, as if the eyes were closed or one were blind, ruminating over them for an uncertain time determined by the reader himself, and no one else. At that exact moment, having seen the sentence, one's appreciation would not be diminished or lowered, if suddenly one could not see. Perhaps, even, it would be enhanced. However, due to the computer's overbearing influence, our perceptions are now essentially visual. I hold that our powers of aesthetic appreciation have decreased, by outside influence, without our knowing that that transmutation and diminution was taking place.

When one reads properly, one alternatively opens and closes one's eye to savor the treats of the author, to enter that far-away world that is his, to imagine Calvino's Italy, Joyce's Dublin, Hemingway's Big Two-Hearted River, and the Fox River up there in the town of Seney in the Upper Peninsula of Michigan. Simultaneously, this experience is private, while at the same time communal, affirming the reader's humanity, if successful, and the artist's art, if it is deft. Such language, privately viewed and contemplated, runs counter to and is a completely different aesthetic or rational event from what the computer offers: Split-second images splashed from a thousand angles with nothing behind the image to ponder. Indeed, that is precisely the point since suddenly, if you are to be the perfect purchaser, there is no Time, and no Space. It does not matter to anyone who designs and maintains computers what you think. Thus, without knowing it, we have all become unwitting pawns in this elaborate game of their creation. It is important only that you are a purchaser, part of the system, and that your mother's maiden-name is already on file so that when you want to buy something, there will not be that dreaded, quite modern word: Glitch.

How times have changed! If you told a counter-culture person (What an inaccurate moniker that turned out to be!) that 25 years later that, for example, to commence regular television reception, a full catalogue of personal datum would be required, he, still pony-tailed, still inclined to deride anything omniscient, would have equally scoffed. Now, to return one's new child from the hospital to the home, say, 3 days after his bloody welcoming to this stage of all life, it is only after the state (how ominous, how ubiquitous!) has assigned the little peeing bugger a social security number. Once again, 25 years ago, how they would have mocked the likelihood of such a controlling proposition, and today how blithely, how seamlessly, we have accepted nearly all of this, and so much more, as the acceptable norm! All healthy skepticism has fled! Whatever happened to skepticism? Who proposed that we must quietly accede to so much? Where is today our latest Bartleby the Scrivener, of Melville fame, who might say to us all,

"I would prefer not to?" Has he been forgotten? Is he disused? Does he no longer count? Can he no longer speak? Has Melville's book not been left the shelf?

Look at what has been largely lost in our pell-mell and haphazard dash toward anything tech. For example, please consider the classic dictum: The four-stage process of discovery:

1. To note,
2. To diagnose,
3. To treat,
4. To revisit.

These are all signs of a mature and rational mind, that entity which may discover and examine a problem, prescribe an antidote and then see if it had clearly worked. All these signs and guideposts of one's maturity are gone, obviated, anticipated by the computer and its designers, so as to effectively render unnecessary the mind itself. That maturity, that is, the ability of a freed mind to think through difficult problems with a singular focus, has been supplanted by a burgeoning computer-driven consciousness in which all desires, wants, and unchartered wishes are suggested, detailed, and delivered by conglomerates that really do know more about us than we know about ourselves. Father John would have surely predicted the disappearance of this four-stage process so crucial to basic diagnostic thought.

My fear is that in our quick embrace of technology, we may have overlooked one proposition: As a man grows older, it is more and more his ability to focus and to concentrate that informs him, and not the quality or speed of his computer. However, what if he has not done that recently, or simply gotten out of the habit? Understand, Ettore? Have computers not made that habit of mind less likely and less plausible? The ability to hold one good thought for a long time is one of the most pleasurable and most private aesthetic experiences one can have. I do not think it is possible to enjoy this type of thing with a computer as a partner. We may have lost our ability to have a vision or to think outside of a box that the computer has made for us. In the process of this fearful embrace, have we not already been circumscribed, circumcised, or gelded?

For a moment, let us focus on the Telemachus portion of James Joyce's Ulysses, and in particular, that book's desultory first three chapters, which, to my reading, are so poignant and so sad, especially in light of the existence of the more vibrant conclusion of A Portrait of The Artist As A Young Man, a book written just prior to the composition of Ulyssess. As a college student five decades ago, I used to wonder what had happened to Stephen Dedalus between the two books, and why and how he had morphed from the supreme artist to the delicate lazy man. Or consider the fevered re-hearing of Mahler's 5th Symphony and always its begged question: Is life to be always this grief-ridden? Ponder the re-seeing of (yes!) The Mona Lisa: What was it that gave La Gioconda's smile such a patient capacity? All these aesthetic experiences are primarily private and repeatable and, further, can be shared with others in discussion and debate, their finer points argued over tea and biscuits or the customary glass of red wine, perhaps a Teroldego. But, during those discussions and debates no one will say to another what or how to think, where to put one's trust and beliefs, and, assuredly, what next to buy.

So, the best marketers in the world have seized upon all new technology as the best fuel for their fast cars, having exhausted autos themselves. Their job (and they have done it oh so brightly!) has been to bring to birth the now common desire, which is 'To be netted'. Accordingly, as parents we give full computer technology to our teenagers, whom we assuredly love, and do not consider that action dangerous. Why would we ever think that such a powerful and separate tool of communication would be a good idea? How many sensitive teenaged minds have been warped by this too early gift?

Further, an entirely new lexicon, downloads, bytes, URLs, and ROMS, ad infinitum has been introduced and assimilated with a numbing quickness by the most eager buyer as if it were the new ABCs. All proper cynicism, any reasoned skepticism, has disappeared. My question is: In those early days, when the computer first arrived on the scene, why was there so little apparent resistance? Why has there been so little contemplation of the possible unintended or harmful consequences of this machine that pretty much thinks for us? May one ask the question today: Do we still know how to think? Will we ever again need to do so? The protected and powerful mavens of the computer world, they have sold to us and sold it well: A whole lot of new soap. Not to be left behind is always the threat! Sometimes, it may be good and fortunate to be left behind, especially if one is lucky enough to traipse along the higher reaches of the Big Belly Mountain of western Wyoming.

I just find this invention meant to secure money and power profoundly unfulfilling. I know that I am mostly alone in this, and do not care one wit or iota. To me, the computer is as satisfying as a cucumber sandwich, low-alcohol near-beer, or very weak and lukewarm tea.

Also, lacking much concept of Divinity, man's innate love of machines has gone too far and over-arched itself. I wonder, if we had more developed spiritual lives, would we find the computer such a welcome friend? When was it exactly that we decided to love machines more than God? Not a bad question to ponder as one blithely clicks away, so blissfully modern, so pointedly non-blessed, caught up in one fleeting and unsubstantial visual image after another. In the evolution of human thought and in our progression away from 'Baser beings', is it not our potential for this 'Lucidity of thought' that sets us so clearly apart? Our ability, if we are to develop it, for a heightened awareness differentiates us from all other consuming animals. How exactly, then, does the computer make it easier for us to think, to focus, to ponder? The point is, it doesn't (although it may make the claim!) since thinking is still left best up to us, as individuals, not it.

In this respect, the computer does not represent a breakthrough for human evolution, however much we are told the contrary, since the hard, dirty, and slow work of focusing, of spiritual progression, of reading distant lucidities must still be done privately in a quiet room or at the end of a long pier. And all of this takes more than a little audacity. I should always try to say or think or write something new, which is something that a computer, however sublime in its construct, cannot accomplish. Nonetheless, often and callously, it is sold on another basis. As the universal panacea for all of life's challenges, including the chance "To be netted, to be made aware." That statement, of course, is hogwash. All in all, we have been sold a half-cooked hash.

Thinking is not a passive process; rather, it is presumptively active: To make oneself aware. In these slights of hand, perhaps made by the jingoistic salesman, the computer becomes not just a beautiful source of old information just newly collected, or another chance for an abject consumer to flex his monetary muscles, but a new form of unguarded power. This new machine is always telling us what to do; it is a new tyranny which one can embrace or rebuff or look askance at as one trundles along, blindly, under so many blinking, costly lights.

Why is it that we cannot seem to prevent, indeed actively encourage, every new fake religion, such as this one, which is simply one more in the long line of others, e.g., the steam engine, the telephone, the television, from becoming such a tyranny? The answer is because we want it to be so, and there is still all that whole lot of new soap to be sold.

All these questions and these observations I recall from that first, long conversation with Father John at the Wilson Ranch on the angled side of the enormous Sulphur Mountain. As a clever and thoughtful man, reading my face as if he were a general reading a map before battle, so many years ago he sparked all these questions in me even then. He had regarded me so comprehensively and, therefore, knew what I was about to say even before I said it. Thus, Father John had warned me well. He, too, was a skeptic; he, too, asked the simple enough question that we are no longer allowed to ask: Why? How do we know that such and such is true and shall last? He too, did not automatically accept anything. He made me challenge my idea that watching Hitchcock was important. He told me that in watching movies, I had become essentially passive, putty. He explained to me that the better the director, the more paralyzed I would become. He ordered me, instead, to develop my brain, my own brain, and through prayer to God's gift of grace for better guidance and direction.

Too, over the intervening years, fellow reader Father John sometimes asked me what books I was reading. I told him once that I was reading most all of Steinbeck, whom I enjoyed because so many of his wry descriptions of workers of the earth mirrored my own simple life working in the fields and orchards. Surprisingly, (although thinking back on it, I ought to have expected his advice), Father John then suggested that since I obviously enjoyed the confessional novel, and that perhaps I would like those written by a myriad of the Russian writers: Dostoevsky, Gorki, Turgenev, Gogol, and Chekhov. He said that I might wish to study the declining fortunes of the Ranevskis in The Cherry Orchard, contemplate the swindler Pavel Chichikov in Dead Souls, or read of the crude materialist Yevgeni Vassilyich Bararov in Fathers and Sons. I had no idea that this self-effacing man was, on the side, in his spare time, next to playing his quite capable golf, a keen student of Russian, or what we now call Soviet, literature.

He explained then that I would be subtly transitioning from the jocular to the psychological; too, he told me that there was much more to learn from failure than success. And as usual, when I did as he suggested, I found out again that he was right. He wanted me to read good stuff, not junk, and understood that in that process, my mind (something in which he had a constant interest) would necessarily and slowly mature. More than anything else, he wanted me to read and to develop permanent relationships with books.

Now, those that dreamt up and then foisted the computer upon us would probably term Father John a throwback, on old fogey, some absent-minded fool, or fanciful pipe dreamer who ought to be ignored. They would righteously castigate him, if he were alive today, as a dowdy chowderhead who fights progress too much. Yet, if I interpret what he said to me so many years ago,

"Read. Don't watch," wasn't he admonishing me to learn how to think, how to better use my piddling brain, and how to develop it well and carefully before something else takes it over?

And, in saying so, so many years ago, did Father John not clearly predict where we would end up? By setting up these false goals, we have necessarily decreased our brains' ability to dissect complex issues. Simply put, computers have made us dumber and lazier. We rely on them to make lame excuses for weak effort, making please for 'glitches' when there are none. We no longer mature mentally as fully as we ought to do. We no longer enjoy the sublime aesthetics of art and music as we used to do. We no longer use our innate capacity for memorization as we once did. We are not as quick as we should be with discovery, diagnosis, treatment, and reassessment, and so, patients and plants, and all sorts of other entities are neglected and accountably suffer. And we can, nevermore, I suspect, hold seven opposing ideas in our heads simultaneously, as F. Scott Fitzgerald says we ought to be able to do.

So, let us ask ourselves: Could we successfully plan D-Day today? Or would we trust all of that intricate and complicated planning for a computer? What if the computer failed? What if it had not been told completely enough exactly what to do? We can, I predict, no longer plan for a storm without running out of ponchos. I suspect that in that computer-planned battle, we would quickly run out of many things: Ammunitions, water, gas, bandages, and, yes, that whole lot of new soap. How does this happen? If one does not use a muscle, it overnight starts to atrophy, to lose mass, to shrink. I think that is where we are today, a place where we are not able to think as well as we should. If one is not used to mental audacity, it seems a foreign concept. To reach across hidden realms of the brain, to make unforeseen connections, it is good that it works well and often, and mostly on its own. I am fearful that in this too-fevered push toward unsuspected and overwhelming technology, we may have lost our minds' most cheerful and crucial capacity, its independence. It is high time we got it back.

Since so many have eloped unconsciously with the computer, that entity which I now call derisively,

"This grand thing," the computer designers have given to it more or less complete power or dominion over our lives. They have happily given themselves up to it. It is not a tool to be used, but something that exerts utter control in this world of ours which, we believe, is the only one. And this is where the crucial fault lies. If those 'computer believers' were to recognize that this life is but a temporary waystation, perhaps they would be less willing to entrust their souls to something so fallible and so enticing made in this world. Accordingly, then, logic would compel those many, once they had taken off 'This grand thing's' prisoner's chains (My apologies to Clement of Rome), to understand and to take to their hearts that,

"The one like a Son of man received dominion, glory, and kingship; all peoples, nations, and languages serve him. His dominion is an everlasting dominion that shall not be taken away, and his kingship shall not be destroyed." (Book of the Prophet Daniel 7: 13–14)

Today I am glad that Father John scouted me out at that fancy party at the Wilson Ranch on Sulphur Mountain since he pointed me in the right direction. As we have witnessed, that afternoon Father John set off a chain reaction of profound thought which shows no sign of diminishment, even after all these days, years, and decades. Thoughts that he instigated in me even while I was still in college continue today to weave and twist and develop themselves. He was a man who knew exactly what he was doing. He wanted to teach and to guide; and so, he did exactly that. He would not be at home in this computerized world, and nor am I. Today he would say, were he still alive, that this thing had been accepted too blithely and had become far too powerful. (May one say this today without getting into hot water?) Therefore, he taught me well, and now that he has passed on, today he may easily smile down on all of us from his well-deserved spot in heaven.

In the beginning, the computer mavens told us that technology was going to be cheap and easy: Two big lies. Now it is used to squash debate; however, as members of a struggling republic, if we do not ask good questions, is there not a price to be paid? Now, via misleading and manipulative algorithms, it is used to skew and manipulate elections. Now it is used to censor differing and divergent opinions in devious and cynical ways never imagined or comprehended. Now it is used to compel teenagers to do this or buy that. Now in the form of social media, it promotes bullying and robs teenagers of their youth. Now it is used to promote harmful pornography, emasculating men, and damaging marriages. For years, twitter was controlled by sneaky devils on the far left and nobody, including those within our collusive government, said one word. We no longer talk to our neighbors, thus harming the social contract. And we think that texting is communication, when, instead, it is akin to talking to yourself in the closet. Yes, I do know that one cannot put the genie back in the bottle; however, when are we going to wake up?

In the meantime, we have become a nation of consultants, gassers, mere talkers, those attached to the easier security of money, the highest of goals. Old-fashioned work and distilled, determined effort are pretty much gone away. Our unquestioned embrace of technology has resulted in a decrease in our mental powers and acuity. Many, congenitally lazy and disinclined toward effort, do not now possess the requisite ability or focus to attack a difficult problem, something which used to be called 'a hard nut', and fix it. Some others see these issues from the outside; however, they can do little but balk to those on the inside, to those that have the power yet shall not fix anything. Those on the inside, still intent on money and power, like things just as they are. So, those on the outside think and say,

"Hey, listen. If you are not going to blow the whistle on this mess, why don't you just step aside?"

During this long battle for the souls of men, it shall be difficult for those on the outside to achieve victory. For that reason, I hold that steady prayer shall be required, if that victory is to be eventually secured.

Twelve years before I met Coach Ferrari, when I was just a drooling piker, hardly a kid, he must have been in battle in Korea. The sinewy, completely in-shape Marine had participated in combat, ate cold rations, fought against the swarming North Koreans, and saw his buddies get their faces torn up and legs shot off. Had he been at the amphibious landing at Inchon in September of 1950? Too, did he endure the intense long hours of cold at the Chosin Reservoir when the temperatures dropped down to minus 35 degrees Fahrenheit? And what did he think about General Douglas MacArthur, AKA Big Doug, getting fired by President Harry Truman for general insubordination on April 11, 1951? However, for the four years that I knew coach he never wanted to talk about any of these military matters, since he did not want to talk about yesterday, but, instead, only about today and tomorrow.

Coach Ferrari

To the north and in the opposite direction from Sulphur Mountain another enormous mountain protects the valley from savage winter storms, and from her apex, if I had made the long trek to the top, I could have seen deep in the center of the valley the red Spanish tile roofs of my new school, where I would spend, studying and exercising, the next four years. And from the first minutes of that first day of the first year, more than a little nervous and cautionary, my fellow students whispered to each other,

"Who the heck is this Ferrari fellow everyone keeps talking about?"

In his unapologetic fierceness, from my first day of high school, when I first saw him, he reminded me of a strict, but ignored, Roman senator who tried to warn the lax and dissolute patricians away from any further ruin. I would soon learn that Coach Elmo Ferrari would tell us not to fritter, not to waste time, to always concentrate on the job at hand, and to finish it completely before moving on to something else. He was full of energy and tightly muscled like a coiled spring. He was intense beyond all description. However, was he too wayward, too acerbic? If so, we, his athletes and students, did not think so, since we, most of us that is, all loved him, since he clearly cared for us and demonstrated that strong emotion to us every day.

Coach did pretty much everything at my high school. He taught Spanish, Ancient History, Typing, and who knows what else. Primarily, he was the Athletic Director, so he coached vociferously, vigorously, completely, all three major sports. Additionally, he bought all the sports equipment, scheduled games and practices, spoke with Tri-Valley League officials about all future events, and stripped the fields with fluffy white chalk before all games. For all of this (and more I do not know about), he was paid a modest sum. However, he did not dismiss or demean the pay, since he fully loved our school, Villanova.

It had been established back in 1924 by the Augustinians, an order long known for its erudition and ability to instruct unfocused and squabbling teenagers. Situated as it was about 75 miles north of Los Angeles, it was set in the bucolic Ojai Valley, which was especially unspoiled at that time, before the powerful real estate interests took hold of the golden state California and slowly strangled her. Ojai is a Chumash Indian word for 'The Nest', a name most apt since encircling the small valley were dozens of 4,000 and 5,000 foot peaks, peaks of red earth covered with chaparral, a dense thicket of shrubs and small trees, toyon, and the darkest red hardwood of manzanita. Every once in a while, once the arroyos and dales and saddles had become dry, a condition usually caused by drought but occasionally by the desiccating blasts of the Santa Ana winds, boring adiabatically down the curving canyons, especially those barrancas lined with plants not burned in scores of years, that impossible thicket, by that time reaching the condition of a highland's dark green blanket, it, she, the heart of the forest, would as if suddenly combust, ignite herself in a fiery, smoking, unstoppable conflagration which might last for days, weeks, before it would subside, spent, with no more tinder-dry fuel left to burn. Usually, the hardworking and the exhausted firefighters contained the burning to the mountains or the foothills, what is called, both in English and Italian, the Piedmont, the foot of the mountain, il piede del monte. But sometimes even there, on the edge of what used to be called civilization, some interloper, some person, unsuspecting and never fearing the worst, would have built the smallest cabin or refuge, and in the face of these fires and despite the endless efforts of the firefighters, routinely they, these tiny huts would be lost, consumed by these most voracious of fires. Afterward, the only thing left would be a lone chimney as a tribute to man's folly or else a mute gathering of small charred and blackened wooden sticks pointing to the still smokey sky.

But most people down below in the valley rarely thought of any of this. Though they had seen the destruction that fires might cause, they rarely thought of them or spent their days afraid of them. If it happens, it happens, or so they thought. As always, life goes on or the ship sails on.

The early priests, Fathers Cantwell and McGrath, and all the others whose names have been lost in the endless passage of time, in those beginning years had selected the rural Ojai Valley as a frontier post of seclusion, the better for the students to more deeply study and to advance spiritually. It would be a place apart from the rapturous stirrings of everyday urban life, a secluded and restful place where their young teenage students, and they themselves as teachers, instructors, professors, guides to the arcane and obvious, might flourish, might grow, might reach a vigorous Catholic manhood the more assuredly, the more graciously.

Many of the boarding students, I soon noticed on those hot days of my first fall there in 1965, were from wealthy and soon-to-be broken homes. Their fracturing parents, working mostly in Hollywood as directors, producers, and the always-present money men, sent their progeny there, up into the mountainous region far from what used to be called the fleshpots of the city, its vacant and costly allure, while the divorce became final, which is, of course, something that could take many years depending always on the attitudes of the two or more attorneys involved and whom they had hired, all of which goes without saying, since today it may be at last admitted that there is no such thing as a speedy divorce.

I noticed too that these boys (not young men, though most of them had begun to shave) always had lots of money in their expensive black calfskin wallets, and sometimes I saw many freshly minted twenties stocked thick there, sporting the likeness of President Andrew Jackson, and afterward, I thought how probably dozens of them were resting there, like a layered green cake setting on a table about to be eaten. I had never seen such a thing! Never! Even to today!

These boys, these boarders, seemed more eager for fun than we 'dayhops'. They had been around; they had seen stuff, and they had attended and enjoyed more than I the various pleasures of the big city. When I compared myself to them, as one inevitably does, the boarders seemed much more mature, experienced, and, particularly when I was surrounded by a whole pack of them, I felt small and weak and like they were in charge, acting as generals, and I was just a mere meager private meant to follow without pause or question their various shouted orders.

Those first days of high school were hard. One had to somehow get one's foot on the ground, to figure out where everything is, especially the bathroom so that whenever you had to do one's business, you didn't have to panic or go around scurrying trying at the last instant to find the zipper.

Even though, just thirteen when the football season started, I was small, almost a midget, yet I was game, not realizing how miniscule I was compared with the rest of the guys. The first day of Junior Varsity football practice, I approached Brother John, a heavily muscled, late-vocation man of religion, and foolishly said to him,

"I'd like to play quarterback," even though I was not able to see over anyone on the team, let alone the huge, marauding defensive linemen. He responded with a wry smile, saying,

"Sure, kid. Five laps. Now. I decide who plays where, not you."

And so, I ran my five laps and learned never to be so impatient with him again.

I spent that first football season getting resolutely hammered, roughed up, beat up. I was a punching bag stand-in; but, even so, I loved it: The comradeship, the travel, the smell of the leather cleats and the wet woolen jerseys especially late in the fall when the first fall rains came. On our endless bus trips out of town for away games where we usually got our clock cleaned, Coach Ferrari would give us each five bucks to spend at a coffee shop; and back in those days of the mid-sixties, before all the chaos and wrangling and bad trouble started, that was enough money for a patty melt, a cup of vegetable beef soup, and a humungous vanilla malt. Coach Ferrari would say to me as I ordered in the cafe,

"You need it, Martin. Surely as anything, you need it all to put some pounds on that skinny frame of yours."

I can still hear Ferrari saying this small speech into my ear; and, even then, after the small and quick meal I still had plenty of money left over to tip the middle-aged waitress and to buy a chocolate bar or two for the long ride home.

I was glad when the season was over because with all the rowdy pushing and shoving on the football field, I had developed a nasty, never-healing sore on the bridge of my nose. My heavy black glasses, a la Clark Kent or Plebe Pointdexter, with all the guys sticking fingers through my one-bar facemask (it was all the school had back then, all we had), had created an always oozing sore there. My nose never healed throughout the whole season since as soon as it started to crust over and get itchy, some new lurking boy would stick his rough, muddy, and probing fingers through my face mask and rip it open again, losing the scab to the ground and making it bleed like gangbusters. And, since his fingers were dirty, the sore would usually get infected and then re-infected. The blood would then flow freely down onto my face and chest and Brother John would ask me if I were OK. I told him that I was fine and that it didn't hurt much. I probably looked like a pirate in a nasty and prolonged battle boarding somebody else's ship. Overall, I was happy when the long football season came to an end, so that we could start in on my favorite game which was basketball.

In my own pea-brain, and notwithstanding my abbreviated height of, say, barely 5 foot 2 inches, I was already in the National Basketball Association, a professional basketball player, one preferably based in Boston, also known as Beantown, and I would play pro ball at the famous and smelly Garden. On this first day of practice, Coach Ferrari had all of us jesters, louts, dweebs, and dingleberries line up, and he bellowed out to us in his usual caustic and extremely loud fashion, saying,

"Show me your hands, your puny and pansy hands. Proffer to me your open fists, please."

He wanted, I slowly gathered, to see who among us might be able because of the large size of his hands to be the better dribbler or disher of the orange pea. But, when he got to me, holding my two narrow wrists in each of his strong, tanned hands, he said,

"Martin, what the hell happened to you? Your hands, why they are so small! Why, I declare that you barely have a thumb! Kid, Mick, you bog-hopper. God must have been in the back having a doughnut when you went through the thumb line!"

Foolishly, like the near idiot that I was, I felt the need to defend my small hands, so I said, countering Seneca's sage advice never to justify oneself,

"I have thick Irish hands, sir, meant for digging with a shovel, something, a tool which we sometimes call 'An Irish spoon'. I have a bog diggers' hands, coach, and that's why they're so thick."

Coach Ferrari responded, saying,

"Thick? Thick? I only care if you can play basketball. Now, let's move on."

Did I notice the smallest sly grin on his face as he continued his review down the line? Today, with this small writing of clear homage to him, I like to think so.

One thing was for sure: Always we practiced with abandon, energy, and endless effort. Coach Ferrari drove us like we were obedient and dogged mules. Maybe we were, or perhaps donkeys, asses. All action was carried out with speed and precision, and the long practices, usually running close to two hours, were organized precisely, as if they were military drills. He expected nothing less than 100% effort from every one of us, down to the last young man. When we were playing defense, he was always talking about the orientation of our hips, the sliding placement of our feet, and that we must be parallel to the offensive player and not perpendicular. We must never have our legs cross over each other since that would take too much time and leave the defender in a desperate and vulnerable position. And one of Coach Ferrari's favorite sayings was,

"Gentlemen, ladies, you can have a bad shooting night, or a lousy offensive effort, when the ball just won't go in the hoop, but you can never, never have a crap defensive performance since a good defense is only and always about effort. Untiring effort! Do you hear me now? You must have the quickest feet and hips, too, know how to slide, glide. Got that? Do you follow? Do you understand?"

At our practices and games, Elmo used very colorful language. He once said to us when we were gathered together, heavily panting after a practice, trying to catch our breath,

"If you guys were boxers, you'd all be tomato cans. Tomato cans! That practice you just concluded was simply pitiful. Pitiful."

He, ex-Marine, cussed all the time, or so it seemed. We loved it since his strident and histrionic hyper-masculine use of the English language made it seem as if he were admitting all of us into his own unique and private military club. Would we then be asked to fight alongside him against the Koreans or the Chinese? For that singular reason, each one of us would not have been surprised if one day he had alerted us to a coming battle and immediately handed us a carbine, a bazooka, or perhaps a hand grenade.

I remember one time when we were playing our biggest rival, Santa Clara, at home in football and they were embarrassing us, Ferrari was beyond it. Every other word was the 'F' bomb. He grabbed Donald Smith, our best athlete by yards, by the facemask and exercised his head like it was a ventriloquist's dummy, using many coarse words that I had never heard before, let alone used. He yelled at Donald, but he was really speaking by extension to the whole, ineffectual team, saying,

"You jerks couldn't find a snowball in a blizzard. Damn! A bunch of coconuts, chicken heart, sissy Marys!"

Later that same day, when he was really 'Using the blue', the Augustinian headmaster came out of the stands to admonish him, stating,

"Coach Ferrari, we have many wealthy benefactors here for the game, and too, students with tender ears. Please watch your language. Please."

Instantly, as if on point, Ferrari responded,

"I tell you what, Father: Why don't you coach the darn team?"

As students with nearly virgin testosterone coursing through our young veins, who could not love an outspoken and unafraid guy like that, one full of unrestrained moxie, grit, and verve?

We knew that he had been a Marine in the Korean War, the Forgotten War as it is sometimes called, but he never spoke about it, even tangentially, and many of us wondered: Had something bad happened to him there, something evil or catastrophic which informed his always thorough fierceness? We knew that he hated communism because one day he said, out of nowhere, or seemingly,

"A friend from Indiana, a state where all the men tell the full and unvarnished truth, told me once and I agree, that Russia is not a place to be desired. Do not ever trust them, the Russian leaders, no matter what the fawning press says. Remember that some of those practiced liars said good things about that evil tyrant, Joseph Stalin. Can you imagine?"

That day, I recall across decades of time that coach had a long-ago, far-away look in his eyes, as if he were thinking of an old girlfriend that had left him for another or of his elderly Italian mother who had died suddenly in a fall. He clearly had thought about these internal issues more than the war itself.

Not long after that, one day he was our substitute teacher for typing class, and suddenly, as was his habit for surprise, he uttered this declaration to the class in the lowest and most serious of tones,

"It was a mistake, a huge mistake, for the American Army to hand Berlin to the Russians. That date was April 1, 1945, or thereabouts. We sat on our asses only 70 miles west of Berlin for a damn month while the Russians, those renegade barbarian Huns, raped the women of Berlin, started fires all over town, sacked the city savagely, stole and looted countless, priceless artifacts, never to be found again. Why? Because we were tired, fatigued? Damn! Do you hear me? Acquiescing, we allowed and permitted the barbaric Huns to seize the city!"

At the end of this long speech, he seemed tired, exhausted, and his deep brown Italian eyes had a glazed look, as if they belonged to someone too long haunted and hunted, some errant fugitive too long on the road and away from a normal life. That lone day in typing class was the closest Coach Ferrari ever got to discussing what he had seen, the vagaries and chaos of the war.

We players noticed that more and more Coach Ferrari seemed to have persistent physical problems. Part of his gradual physical dissolution, his always being tired or suddenly weak, was attributable to the well-known, yet barely mentioned fact, that he was an unstable diabetic. Often during practice, he would become suddenly weak, and then he would swoon to a near-coma. His blood sugar was nearly always out of whack, and often he would bark or rasp to Dave Simmons, our class's finest athlete, saying,

"Simmons. Get me an orange. Now. Please. Simmons! Simmons! Or you, Ramos! Ramos! Please. Now!"

So, after that first day, we would keep on hand a whole crate, a full 40-pound lug box of fresh oranges for him. They were already sliced in half, so that whenever he needed one, it would already be cut in two, quickly available for him to eat. Acutely ravenous for the sugar, the sweet orange juice would then drip messily down his chin, dropping to the ground.

He was handsome, yet suffered greatly, in a deep and apparently unspoken loneliness, since, apparently, he could neither find, nor retain, a woman. Though small, he had the kind of super athletic stature whereby he could easily have been a major league infielder, someone like a Jim Gillian or a Charlie Neal, who both played for the Los Angeles Dodgers, someone with the quickest hands and the most scampering of feet. Whenever he felt well, fit, sharp, which wasn't that often, he would bound up into the air, bound skyward like a deer, a young gazelle. Regarding women, I think now that maybe he was too fierce, too intense, and too obdurate to adapt himself to become the more nurturing type inclined to steadfastly love a woman. Had the war in Korea made him so, marked him for this mean and constant austerity forever? I knew that he was not some closeted pansy because every day he made an appropriate, slightly leering, or comic salute to the beauty of the female form or the surprising banality and unforeseen hilarity of physical union. Whenever he said these manly things, he always had a different or tired look in his Madagascar brown eyes, like he was weary well beyond normal from another long and lonely bus ride, and that, deep in his heart, he already understood or knew it, that a happy marriage would probably never be in the cards for him.

Some years passed, and I unwittingly, eventually, became an upperclassman. Though still small, weak, and pimply, I tried to make up for those considerable faults with an unguarded determination, particularly on the ball field or court. Also, at the same confounded time, drugs arrived on our campus with their false yet unquestioning seal of approval from most of society's self-appointed bigshots. By those arrogant warlords dominating our culture, such as it then was, drugs were instantly considered chic, and the boarders and all others who lolled about who had the cash to do so, purchased them and instantly became unintelligible or worse, catatonic. Yet the exuberant popularity of the drugs not only persisted but increased. LSD, whose full chemical name is lysergic acid diethylamide, was praised by the famous but completely bonkers Dr. Timothy O'Leary as the panacea for all of life's problems, and it instantly, overnight (or so it seemed) became the drug of choice, or at least for those self-praising drug-loving cognoscenti in the know. Many of my trusting classmates unsuspectingly took him at his jaundiced word. And many of my fellow students partook of it, during those halcyon days of the late sixties, apparently never thinking that it might be injurious to:

1. The heart,
2. The mind,
3. The body,
4. The psyche,
5. One's possible manhood, or
6. All of the above.

So, it was no big surprise that one day at the start of basketball season for my junior year, much to the chagrin of the school's higher officials who were at first unable to check or slow the drug's relentless rise in fashion, when an ambulance arrived: Why? One of my fellow students and a fellow basketball player, clearly not using the good brain that God gave him, had ingested a tab of LSD.

How much? What form? From whom had the dangerous tab been purchased?

Inevitably, all sorts of wild rumors flew. It turned out that the reckless imbiber had embarked onto what was then called a 'Bad Trip', something then considered truly unfortunate and regretful. It later was made clear that Paul Hickey (not his real name, since what short purpose would such a defamation serve?) during his bad trip saw in his mind only mean, consistent visions of snakes coming in and out of his head. Those snakes migrated out of his mouth, out of his ears, near to his tongue, which, I was later told, moved furtively about his mouth endlessly, like many of those same snakes looking for food, water, prey.

When I heard of this sad and painful case that beset one of my fellow students, one just one year younger than I, I asked myself, as I am sure many other students did,

"Why do we subject ourselves to such proscribed onslaughts? Why do we ask our unsuspecting bodies to endure, to digest, and to detoxify such foreign and unknown substances? And why do we routinely make the false assumption that so many of those compounds (made by whom and guaranteed by what unknown stranger?) will be safe?"

But I then checked myself since I did not feel superior or supercilious toward Paul. We had played many sports together, and I respected, indeed, envied his obvious robustness and skillful co-ordination which was much superior to mine. Had it not been for my innate fear of the twists of fate, I thought then, I too might have joined him in his unguarded, unhappy voyage.

As I recall (and I may be inaccurate at this juncture, since so uncertain or loose is the grip of my memory upon certain clear facts of the past, long-gone events which become the more unknowable however much one squints into the past's mists or yearns to know them better) Paul dropped out of our school, and I never saw him again. Following a growing pattern seen so often in my youth and given the ascending drug-fueled distractions of society, suddenly I had scores of friends who then mysteriously departed, never to be seen again.

That Friday's basketball practice, coming right after Paul Hickey's bad LSD trip, Coach Ferrari was steamed, riled, clearly off his nut. I truly thought that he might explode or blow a gasket! He was simply gone and over the moon with anger. All through practice, he was steamed, railing, nearly doubled up with strong and penetrating emotion. He was normally suitably on edge, but that day he was over the edge, almost apoplectic, vigorously energized, and yet on point. He was like a high hurdler just before the race: Coiled, tense, and pissed off at the entire lousy world. Why not? After a short but intense practice, he told us to gather around, shut our open, gapping mouths, and take a knee on the maple floor in the corner of the gym. Waiting a good speaker's second or two or three, to secure and guard our attention, and to gauge his audience's tone and settling demeanor, he began one of the most important speeches that I have ever heard in my entire life, saying,

"Did you, numbskulls see what Paul Hickey did today? Do you also want to go down that meathead path? You can, you know it, wastrels; you can do so! It is a perfectly easy thing to mess up your life, just like our friend, Mr. Hickey, did. So, let me ask you: Do you wish to follow him, like he is some kind of phony pied piper? Do you allege that he is another Rasputin? Are you sheep that gladly jump off a Dorset cliff into the steaming sea because the others do?"

He continued in full, elevated froth, continuing to deliver one of the finest, keen, and sharp harangues I have ever heard anywhere, proclaiming,

"This weekend is a test for each one of you knot heads, you dunderheads, and this afternoon I truly wonder whether you shall pass the examination. Are you guys going to be squirt away this weekend or what? All of life is a test, boys. All of you must be born ready, understand? So, if you use drugs like LSD, if you smoke anything, if you drink anything stronger than lemonade, if you race cars, if you steal bourbon out of your dad's bourbon bottle, if you try anything untoward with girls, if you disrespect your parents, if you miss Mass on Sunday morning, if you ever even flipping cuss within earshot of old people, on Monday afternoon, at this same blooming practice, I shall know the truth, just by looking for a second at your dumb and surly faces, and then I'll kick your ass. Hard. And repeatedly. Is that fully understood? Your life will soon become manifestly ugly? Do you understand me? Am I suitably clear? I say all of this to you empty-headed whelps, you unaware tubs of lard, you empty-headed loafers because it is simply my job, one given to me by God alone, to do so. Now, get out of here, and I'll see you Monday afternoon at 3:15, and I mean sharp. Sharp!"

When he said that last word, 'sharp', Ferrari's whole hard body stiffened further, like he was having a full-on heart attack or something. Right away I knew in my gut that Coach Ferrari's long speech would never be forgotten since it would be pivotal and key for the rest of my life. Finally, a few seconds later, coach relaxed, and I could see in his eyes a long and distant look, like he was not there at all, but somewhere else in his mind, maybe back at some faraway muddy Korean battlefield, some place dismal, grim, cold and unpredictable, someplace sloppy with mud where his buddies had been killed by Communists who hid behind bushes or in a trench. Or perhaps he was thinking about some dark and freezing barracks where certain uncontrolled and horny men cannot stop talking about nookie even though there is absolutely none around anyway and where there was always that strange dude from Indiana who kept making oblique comments like this one,

"Russia is not desirable."

Even today I still reflect upon Coach Ferrari's words, knowing that he cared about each of his players, and that he did not want any of us, not one, to go down that popular, but faulty, perditious road of drugs.

A week later, just after the football team had their final home game of the fall season, and with that, their homecoming dance wherein the gym floor had been treated with a coat of wax, Coach Ferrari was leading us in practice, and specifically, basketball agility drills. By that time, over the course of the previous summer, I had grown quickly taller, to well over 6 feet. Unfortunately, I was so uncoordinated and awkward that when I went to brush my teeth, I often hit my left ear with the toothbrush. Too, when I tried to navigate through a doorway, I would usually slam one of my shoulders, sometimes the left, occasionally the right, into the door jamb. So, then, it was no surprise that day at practice, while Coach Ferrari was leading us in agility drills, telling us to quickly shift our feet left and right, forward and backward, that I should get my long, skinny legs tangled up with each other and fall, cascading like a lump of laundry down a tall laundry cute, with me falling hard down to the maple flood. Unfortunately, I used my outstretched open right hand as an Elmer prop so I would not fall head-first or so hard, and then, toward the end of that unexpected falling action, if I had been paying proper attention, I might have heard the smallest click or snap of the bone, my radius, as it broke into two pieces, like a breadstick or grissini does, at the start of a meal. The clean fracture was quite close to the wrist, which suddenly hung limply as if were entirely disconnected from the rest of my pink and now-swelling arm. Years later I would discover that I had suffered the common Colles' fracture, after an Irishman from Kilkenny, and one that typically results from an unexpected fall, with all the falling weight borne by that outstretched hand.

It hurt terribly. The pain seared at me and instantly made me feverish and nauseous. Within seconds, I pucked, all over the floor, partially hitting the coach's tennis shoes with my freshly minted vomitus.

Coach Ferrari was immediately steamed, seething, apoplectic with rising anger. And then he said,

"Dammit, Martin. Clod! Who must clean that mess up? Me! Knute Rockne asked the pertinent question: You have only two feet. Do they have to step on each other? And I tell you what, buster: You break that thing again, you'll have to get the son-of-a-bitch pinned."

When he said the crucial word 'pinned' his eyes became intense, like a Navy pilot's would be just before a dogfight in the sky. And it was just at that quick instant that I realized that all the guys on the basketball team, well, we loved this intense, competitive, and demanding guy, we really did, since he really cared about every one of us.

So obviously, that injury ended that basketball season for me. I had a cast on for four long months and can still recall the stinky, bad cottage cheese smell in the palm of my right hand because I could never clean it there. The rancidness grew and never went away. Eventually, after it had gotten spongy and lumpy from errant moisture, the cast came off, and I was shocked to see how weak my entire right arm appeared. It looked like a sick chicken or inconsequent eel. There was hardly any muscle there anymore, and the skin on my right arm was a sickly color of ocher or immature plaster. Eventually, though, with time, it grew slowly stronger and at the end of that junior year, in strength it was almost equal to the left.

It was then time for another year, my last. Finally, we were seniors, the Big Shots on campus, or the true and manly gladiators, paid mercenaries, or so we thought in our eager minds. All I thought about was basketball, or almost. In my fanciful mind, once again I figured that I really should be in the NBA. I practiced endlessly, both at school and on my own. In my own small, pixelated brain, I was a superior player, capable of great offense, tenacious defense, and, a sacrificing player full of team play, assists, and hustle, one whose copious skills need only be refined, not developed, since I was already a star.

All of this was, of course, raucous or savage fiction. I was barely mediocre, or even less than that, poor. I could not score and had little upper body strength to rebound well. And thus, the short tableau that follows should come as no small surprise.

Ferrari had approached me the day before a game early in the season with that familiar steely glint to his steady brown eyes. He told me,

"Martin don't ask me why, but I'm going to start you against Moorpark. Probably a huge mistake, but, what the hell. Get ready; do you hear me? Ready!"

I had smiled a little, grinned, not at the news of my starting the game, but thinking as all pubescent teenagers must, that 'Moorpark' is 'Kraproom' spelled backward, and Ferrari, seeing the beginning of my smirk, bellowed,

"Do you think this is funny? Dammit! I'll bench you right now if you want!"

"No, coach. Please don't do that. I was thinking of something else. Sorry."

"Focus, Martin. You would do well to focus."

And he stomped off, fuming, muttering stifled and unheard words down the hallway to his cramped office in the dingy gym.

So, that next night, with my parents in the stands along with a possible tentative, soon-to-be-gone girlfriend whose name and face and shape I can only scarcely recall, I started at center. Butterflies impeded my performance and sent it to a level even lower than normal. Thus, within a mere 10 ticks of the clock, I had committed five major errors:

1. A turnover,
2. Allowing my opposite to score,
3. A failure to rebound an easy ball,
4. Again allowing my opposite to score,
5. And the worst, stepping on the out-of-bounds line while bringing in the ball.

Unsurprisingly then, after such a dismal and brief performance, I was yanked. Ferrari grabbed me by my shirt, shook me some as if I were a limp ragdoll or a blanket full of grey dust, and yelled at me vociferously, asking me the key question:

"What the hell were you thinking?"

Seating me next to him on the humble pie pine bench, he turned toward me and bellowed in a voice as loud as I had ever heard,

"Martin, you're an idiot. No, a king-sized idiot!"

And extending his right middle knuckle outward, he gave me a decisive knock on my temple. He was right! I didn't care one whit if he did! He was right! I watched the guy who replaced me to see how my play might improve. And I thought of that line from the Bible that,

"Sometimes the mind is willing, but the body is weak."

And I thought to myself: *Maybe I shall not be drafted high by the NBA after all.*

Finally, the season passed. I had averaged less than 2 points per game. My rebounding had improved slightly, and I had earned a no-bull reputation for setting good picks, quick and effective defense, scampering after all loose balls, and relentless hustle. Our team, despite our non-stop knockdown efforts, decent defense, and coach's constant and fevered haranguing, had won only 4 games out of 25. Consequently, most of us were silently glad when the games ended, and the season was over, so that the baseball and track seasons might commence.

Further months passed. Graduation gradually drew close, loomed. Soon, this precious and rare universe, where we had studied Latin conjugations, Shakespeare's intent in Julius Caesar, and St. Augustine's anguish at the beginnings of sin, would be no longer. Soon we would have to leave it all: Those hallowed, reverberating hallways which had their own peculiar smell, those ratty ball fields with patches of weeds or bare dirt, and those disordered and smelly locker rooms were never to be seen or smelt again. Then, and always, for a second, I wished that I might have stayed there at Villanova, perhaps to remain a Peter Pan type of fellow apart from the aged rashness of the world and all its future betrayals. Yet, that was not possible, that much I certainly knew, and soon we would all have to take the slow, overland route to the outside world, one hostile and frank, full of deceptions and lies, and then to be alert to all the possible and precipitous dangers which there shall surely lurk.

Graduation day: There it was again, and on through the ages to today and beyond, one that anyone may recall from negligent memory, if there is a desire to do so. That momentous day, Coach Ferrari approached me, and immediately I thought of his fiery, over-the-top Paul Hickey speech (since you never forget a hickey), about how spitting angry he had been that day at Hickey's foolish ingestion of the LSD. Yet, that's not quite right either since all he was trying in his Korean War, Marine Corps kind of way was to protect or shield us from the unseen ugliness and growing undetected evil of the world.

I thought of all of this and more as he approached closer to me. I thought that he had forgotten me, that I was only one of hundreds of other inconsequential dweebs, rubes, so-so Joe Blows, but, unexpectedly, I was wrong, per usual.

With a leatherneck's raucous smile, he surprised me and said,

"Martin, one more time, please, show me your hands. Please."

What a request! The inopportune question was an exact repeat of nearly 4 years ago. I offered my still-small paws to him, and he said to me,

"Hey, but they are still small. I knew it! And, where's the thumb? Maybe you're going to be a late bloomer. But, buddy, I always liked your hustle. Goodbye."

In my four years at the school, those were the first words of faint praise that I received from Coach Ferrari; but that was not a problem since I never expected to receive praise from him. And that word terminal word, 'Goodbye'. His pronouncement of it caught me up, and for a moment I felt within me that tears were close to brimming to the surface. I thought to myself: *It is all so sudden and so final.* Would I ever see him again? Would any of us? What would happen to all of us? He would no longer be around to guide us and to tell us when we were full of crap or puck, which was often.

Now, over the more than five intervening decades, I look back, as one does, at Coach Ferrari. They do not make much like him anymore. Yes, he was pushy, and demonstrative, but so what! Today, coaches cannot rail like he did, and they cannot bellow, touch, paint, gesticulate, curse, intimidate, or demean a player, however much any of these forms of coercive force and direction might be required in a given situation. Thus, students are indefinitely laxer, coddled, entitled, and inevitably spoiled. Since, how does a 17-year-old dingleberry know his own faults and mistakes unless he is told so by an acerbic and demanding coach like Coach Ferrari?

Today it makes me happy and briefly proud to know that Coach Ferrari, on that almost forgotten last day of graduation decades ago, saw me and determined, even though I possessed an obvious paucity of athletic talent, that I was a digger and that I would not quit, ever; and that is one of the finest memories any person can ever have. Coming from him, whom we all so revered, that final conversation between us amounted to a kind of benediction, a word stemming from the Latin word: 'Benedicere', meaning to bless or speak well of. I miss him. I wish he were still around. I want him again near me so that he can again tell me what to do, saying to me in loud, simple, and clear words exactly what it is that I ought to do. It was only years after I had left the school, years after Coach Ferrari had died, that these fleeting reminiscences, filtered through the mists of unstable memory, came back to me so that I might quickly put them down on paper, so that they would not disappear forever.

And so, I graduated that day, leaving the school that had been my fine home for four years. And watching guard over the ceremony was the large mountain to the north, acting like a minister presiding over the actions of the valley. And as the scene drew to its inevitable close, and as the large crowd of parents and graduates began to disperse, and knowing that all would soon change irretrievably, I had this strange and surprising thought: *Whenever one is at our high school deep in the center of the valley, one can look upward and straight north toward the receding mountains and see there the many scarred canyons of toyon and manzanita, the dried rivulets, the bright green trace of cottonwoods that cling to a creek bed.* In the higher reaches, lone pines dot the mesas and infrequent saddles. However, they do not grow well in the oft-polluted air, and, once they are so weakened, many later succumb to the Western Pine Beetle. I thought how hardly anyone knows the name of this enormous mountain which dominates the sky to the north, as a lord or trustee might at a wake, but not because it is a difficult one to pronounce since it is simply called: 'Pine Mountain', or, if the Spanish is preferred: 'Montana Pino'.

Most of these fancy schools have been expensive for decades, which makes perfect sense since they cater to the financial elites who run our country. I am talking, of course, about the colleges of the Ivy League, which has long been a place where the well born go to secure greater financial security later in life. At these well-praised institutions of learning, the primary goal is not to teach and encourage debate and the skills of a logician, but to engender, guard, and pass down to future students the network, that vast assemblage of financial connections that range across space and time, so that the graduates and their offspring in turn might secure as old age approaches prodigious wealth and permanent riches.

However, when these colleges and universities were instituted centuries ago, they purported to claim a distinctly Christian foundation, which in many cases was undeniably true. Indeed, some of them even today display college mottoes which claim a reliance upon the divine. However, five decades ago, with the twin onslaught of the sexual revolution and the arrival of the recreational drug culture, nearly all those moral strictures perhaps inevitably slipped away under the waters. Unfortunately, with time's passage, these once hallowed schools have resolutely turned their back to their own moral histories. Indeed, many of the leaders of these institutions seem embarrassed by Christianity and its firm framework of right and wrong. This same regrettable trend can also be seen in many Catholic universities, places of learning which have also forsaken their past moral template. Moral ambiguity is now the new norm, within both the Ivy League and private schools which once were religious in both tone and content.

The upshot is that professors at these schools are in a bind, especially if they consider themselves to be truly Christian. They are swimming upstream against very heavy currents. Most, in my view, demur and are silent, not wishing to intrude upon the rampant, outlandish fantasies of their students. Too, those professors reasonably adhere to the sensible notion that their pensions and health care plans need to be protected. And in this regrettable process, it is the foxes, the young and often mindless students, who are minding the chicken coop. This undesirable situation has been in place for five decades.

Cows, Cowed

--- There's right and there's wrong. You have got to do one or the other. You do the one and you're living. You do the other and you may be walking around, but you're dead as a beaver hat.

--- Republic. I like the sound of the word. It means the people can live free, talk free, go or come, buy or sell, be drunk or sober, however they choose. Some words give you a feeling. ... Some words can give you a feeling that makes your heart warm. Republic is one of those words.

Two speeches from the Davy Crockett character, played by John Wayne, taken from the film, The Alamo (1960), produced and directed by John Wayne, with a screenplay by James Edward Grant.

Within our nation, if not around the world, free speech has not been exercised on college campuses for five decades, of that one may be certain. Bold candor is gone. Can I say this? May I eat a peach? Will I get in messy trouble for voicing my opinion? Perhaps I am no longer allowed to speak. And the sad fact remains that the leaders, the administrators and professors of those institutions, so thoroughly praised back in the day for their encouragement of free and vigorous discussion, do not seem desirous of a return to open debate, despite what their respective charters may suggest and promise.

In the beginning, when I first stepped onto the beautiful campus, I was so hopeful, so supremely hopeful, that the school would be a place of solid learning. I thought that it, then such a highly revered school, would be different than it turned out. The university was supposed to be one of the best in the land, the sort of school where improper cant was debunked before it was spoken, where precise scholarly excellence was insisted upon, and where heavy and difficult burdens of academic work would be taken for granted. I suppose my new home for the next two years was considered a second cousin or poor stepchild to the grander, older bastions of the Ivy League. As I entered those prestigious grounds that Fall of 1971, only 19, barely shaving, "still wet behind the ears," to use an old phrase, for my first few tenders weeks I definitely felt it a distinct privilege to be there, to be in those rare classrooms, to hear those excellent, scholarly teachers from Oxford and Cambridge and Yale and Princeton expand upon their complex ideas and arguments which I, up until that time, had scarcely broached.

Yet, in that first tentative month, little did I know then that the primary intent of the school was not to educate the student but to culturally transform him. Spiritually speaking, her aim, gathering together all the factors that might be amassed, from the teachers, the students, the conversations in hallways or at the endless parties—the school's spiritual aim was the diminishment of any faith in the divine, and further, to tell me and to insist by the way, that not only was my conventional God dead, but that He had never been alive; and finally, that it had been most foolish of me or anyone else to have thought otherwise.

Yes, I do grant the kind reader that it is common, if not obligatory, to be critical of one's college years, especially with the accumulating passage of demon time, by making broadsides against others of that time (I was smarter than they then) or by engaging in the trap of self-delusion (I was dumb then, too, but today I am so much smarter), since we all tend to falsify our educational histories in their retelling. Embellishments may be the correct word. Seen through decades of misty memory it is no wonder that exaggerations of the most extreme sort often become customary. Some would say that such mock judgments do little harm and are part of the unavoidable process of age. So, if they are so inevitable, what else can be profitably said?

Just as a once-sickly person, newly well, suddenly appreciates the happy mundane aspects of life, its pleasant routine, so, too, a new graduate will thank his parents for their gift of university life to him only shortly before their passing. Early on, most say, amid the nervous exams, the difficult orals, the tedium of all study, that college life is one to be flown from. Then later, perhaps incrementally, it becomes a sacred and mysterious time, even precious. One yearns for it though it be gone. How and why does this looking backward habit so customarily happen?

Viewed from today's vantage, it is easy to say that the university I attended should have been a splendid experience. Was it all it could have been? Was it? All those ideas so well expressed, all those parties to which all were invited, all those near women ostensibly so pliant! There were the grand expectancies of the future, its promise held before us, glittering, like a strong candle in the wind, keeping us forever in its thrall. The world beckoned and it said to me and all the others: Come to me, you silent youth! Come!

And, of course, there were negligible responsibilities. A few papers to be written, a few novels to be read, but, really, very little difficult work was required. In a way the place could be considered a country club, one with negligible responsibilities, and convenient amusements. This was in the beginning days of our collegiate transformation from rigor and rote to freedom and a release from what was suddenly viewed as the earlier, confining structures. Prior strenuous curricula were discarded, summarily dashed onto the tip. One unhappy upshot of that massive curriculum change was that soon English majors (like I was) would no longer be required to study Shakespeare, since, after all, he remains a dead, white guy. This was in those first heady days of presumed emancipation wherein the young student, it was determined, though barely driving, ought to be free to cast about academically according to his own interest, and not the university's. Accordingly, across the country, but especially at the 'fancy' colleges, like mine, prior academic standards went away, like crepe paper bunting dropping away from the bandstand after the party is over. The young student was no longer told what to do, since, for the first time in history, he could choose and design his own course of study. Further, it was no longer an option for any teacher to demand performance. Hope, yes; demand, no. And also, many colleges were right on the edge of introducing baloney majors like Chicano Studies, Black Studies, and Queer Studies. Finally, all of these drastic and foreboding changes at the university took place virtually overnight, watched over by passive administrators who did little but cash their fat paychecks.

As I gaze back into the dim past, some teachers there were most memorable, or, I should more precisely say, memorable to me. Other fellow students today no doubt recall other professors as more salient. For me, Professor Goff's irony while unfolding the obliqueness of Wittgenstein, Professor Hummel's appreciation of Camus' love of the Algerian sun and sea and women, and the gently smiling Professor Grana's explication of the revolt of the masses, all these subtle and nuanced explications remain strong memories for me today. What a cascading swirl of ideas spun all around me for those brief privileged days! And there were always pitchers of Bass Ale and delicious provolone sandwiches, grilled, among the cheap fare on Friday night downtown at a crowded and noisy bar called 'The Catalyst'.

We have the time and leisure to say now that those were glorious days. Yes, they were! For the first six weeks of my final year at the college, for that brief time, I lived in my van, which carried a lumpy bed in the back, parking at various spots along the ocean at night for a disquieted sleep. The police came to know me well, and, since I was neither drug-addled nor a drug dealer, fortunately they left me alone. I showered at the gym and ate, as is a college student's wont, whenever the opportunity arose, i.e., sporadically. Truth be told, I went to parties mostly for free food, free beer, and to meet girls, not necessarily in the order. However, alas, in that later quest, I was distinctly not successful, but not for want of trying.

Still, I never felt alone. Rather, I believed, since we were so consistently taught it, that I belonged to a strongly elitist club whose members were very smart, and further, subtly delighted at the exclusion of all those who were unwanted. The place was a grand club to which many were not invited. And for those invited there was this understood hierarchy of inclusion, coached in a conforming atmosphere of liberal politics, easy hedonism, and unrestrained pleasure. Despite what I had been promised by promotional literature, free speech was frowned upon and pressure to conform to the dozens of progressive mandates was constant, unspoken, and enormous.

Therefore, self-appointed leaders of the club would ask all: Do you all like Angela Davis? Of course, you do! (By the way, I used to see her walking with Huey Newton on the long wooden bridges spanning the broad barrancas and arroyos, and the two seemed to me to be an amatory pair, only having eyes for each other, as well as I can recall). Too, the leaders of the club would pose the query,

"Don't you think that marijuana should be legalized with all the other drugs? What do you think of raising taxes on the rich?"

Most all of these political barometers were left unsaid, said in a low, sotto voce tone, or voiced behind the scenes. It was always assumed in group discussions that everyone held to the identical progressive views, which comprised our marching orders, ones not be contravened; and, of course, this was a practiced and clearly intentional form of intimidation. Thus, on purpose, free speech was already, fifty-two years ago now, starting to depart. The college was simply a propaganda machine, one where we all should march in lockstep, or so it was whispered. Occasionally, I said to myself: Where do I fit in? Who will help me? There are more powerful people than I. They assume way too much. Who among all of them will help me, the weaker? This subcutaneous wondering was nearly unconscious, I now reflect.

With the passage of time, I now understand that most of the students and many of the teachers did not love our country; in fact, they actively cultivated and maintained an active hatred for it. Simply put, the university helped to grow that hatred. Anyone who said that they loved our country or respected authority or laws was instantly made to feel small. Patriotism was an anachronism, something to be scoffed at, as was a belief in the traditional family, a husband and a wife, faithful to each other, heterosexual, with a few children to boot. Thus, traditional marriage was something to be made fun of, castigated, and ridiculed, since it would necessarily hinder wider carnal wanderings. Such crass, untoward extravagancies of thought as these swirled around me. Such foolishness was engendered, promoted, and encouraged daily by left leaning profs who themselves led lives outside the mainstream of the Judeo-Christian history.

Further, to be a practicing, if not vigorous, Catholic at the university provided the easy opportunity for some unanticipated high camp. I quickly grasped one clear fact: Largely surrounded by actively anti-religious views, one could not use the notion of Faith as a defense on any issue. Such an attempt would have been, and was, simply laughed at by the fellow students, many of whom were at least culturally Jewish. For the first time in history, traditional religion did not predominate any discussion within our classrooms. Most of my fellow students considered a religion of any stripe as an afterthought, something for old and feeble people only, those close to the grave, to chew upon. Indeed, no matter what the audience, to attempt to use an irrational Faith in any intellectual argument was to encourage the sharpest derision, bordering on scattering laughter and catcalls. The teachers, it should be noted, were also largely condemnatory toward these predictable arguments of Faith, but their eyes were softer and their tone less aggressively mocking.

There was one outlier. As a caveat, if a student hailed from the Far East or had adopted a religion from that part of the world, say, to have become a Hindu or Buddhist, well then, in that case, all was forgiven, and religion was fine. Their religions were never put down, not that I ever witnessed. During class discussions, newly arrived practitioners of one of those eastern religions were considered suave, sophisticated and with-it; indeed, they were listened to assiduously, as if each were Marco Polo returning from distant eastern shores, talking about exotic teas or the enchanting dance of delicate-limbed Asian women.

Further, it was assumed that all were vegetarian. Only certain types of peanut butter could be purchased. More than once I was asked the question,

"Is the cheese rennet-less?"

Predictably, I began to lose weight. Brown rice, with the odd mushroom or green pea added, was our usual meal. We would pool buy all staples. If one suggested purchasing a nice flank steak, perhaps one quickly grilled and served with cilantro, coarse pepper and much cold beer: Oh! the disliking stare and nasty glances one would receive, looks saying,

"You aren't vegetarian! I can't believe it!"

Much brown rice was eaten, so carefully did we avoid normal American patterns of eating. I now grasp that that low-protein diet was a symptom of other patterns of rejection. It must have been during the Christmas break of my final year that I returned home, and when my mom first saw me, she was shocked at my sharp loss of weight, and asked,

"When was the last time you ate a steak, son?"

And I answered her by saying,

"Mom, I cannot spell that word, steak."

Of course, it scarcely needs to be added that illegal 'recreational' and unchecked sex were everywhere. The chaotic situation recalls a quote from Raymond Chancler's book, <u>Farewell, My Lovely</u> (1940) when he writes,

"I guess that I'm just old-fashioned from the waist up."

In those heady and halcyon days, so universally praised by those in charge, it was simply impossible to know where any moral lines were drawn. Essentially, there were none. To a group so intent on giving up the old traditions of religion, and attendant morals and dicta, it was highly unlikely that they would instantly adopt any new ones.

An apocalyptic story comes to mind: One night at a party in front of scores of people, I, holding a beer, saw two men, one of whom had carefully washed and combed luxuriant brown hair well past his skinny shoulders, kissing each other hard on the mouth. It seemed that they were in real, or what passed for it, passion. I understand now that this unasked-for display was a cool cultural show or performance to which I was lucky to have been invited. Today I reckon that these two young men must have considered themselves liberated and proud of their outside-of-the-mainstream yearnings.

Another vignette presents itself: I recall today a very beautiful blonde, statuesque and ironic, who lived next door. Her appearance was quite stupendous, since her frank voluptuousness was breathtaking and quite beyond description. Unfortunately, she had gotten into the luckless habit of having new sleepover boyfriends, mostly black, in very rapid fashion, as rapid no doubt as their fervently loveless couplings. Though her catalogue of boyfriends was a long one, I still, and impossibly, yearned for her. At that time quite shy, I never tossed my hat into her ring. Now I wonder what aberrant forces pushed her to such harmful extremes. Today I wonder whatever happened to her and her less amatory, more academic aspirations.

Having given up one religion as vestigial and impulse-restraining, weren't we simply looking for others, more exotic, to supplant the old? Did I think that then? Clearly, we would not, then, have called the reckless drug-taking (which I, protesting lamely, eschewed) a new-style religion; but, looking back on those years at college through time and ego-bolstering revision, isn't that exactly what it had become? The administrative leaders of the state university did little or nothing to stop the ubiquitous culture of drugs, despite many suicides of their students, their apparent charges. Weren't all the other phony attempts, e.g., the sex without commitment, the embrace of everything Eastern, the debunking of capitalism in all its forms, etc., were not these predictable efforts simply new, frail attempts at engendering a new religion, although one not to be so called? In the end we must ask the next question,

"Were we not simply trying to tell our parents to go to hell? And Christ?"

* * *

—The outstanding thing about China's 600 million is that they are 'poor and blank'. On a blank piece of paper free from any mark, the freshest and most beautiful characters can be written, the freshest and most beautiful pictures can be painted.

Mao Zedong (1893–1976)

I have included this quote from the Chinese Communist leader since it illustrates what has taken place in our colleges and universities. Though most of my fellow students were distinctly not 'poor', they were 'blank', in the sense that they had already repudiated whatever moral foundation that they might have inherited from their parents, other relatives, and other mentors, like teachers and coaches. They were 'blank pieces of paper free from any mark'. As such, they were quite susceptible to following errant ideologues, might be easily manipulated into all sorts of trouble and vice, and therefore, could easily be talked into hating this country and becoming Marxists.

* * *

Ernest Hemingway in his famous short story "The Gambler, the Nun, and the Radio", speaks of the need for people to find some sort of opiate: Religion, music, economics, patriotism, sexual intercourse, drink, the radio, gambling, ambition or a belief in any new form of government. Although we would not have admitted it at the time, isn't that precisely what we at the much-praised institution of higher learning (sic) were up to?

The skeptics of old-fashioned Faith were everywhere. As a Catholic, albeit then a lackadaisical one, it was both discouraging and illuminating to hear the constant cruel broadsides made against the Papacy, the extreme invectives against 'bad priests', the mean, ruler-wielding nuns, the manifest failure of the Inquisition, the imperialistic underpinnings to the crusades, and the like. Then, much caustic hatred was in speakers' eyes, and, I fear, today it remains in their hearts. In the classroom, that architect of American discourse, if it is to grow, normal civility had disappeared overnight, as a water hole desiccates if there is not a weekly rain. Looking back on those conversations, not restricted to the classroom, today I regret I was not more forceful in defending (a la Ulysses' Leopold Bloom and his Jewishness) my own Faith.

Can the taking of drugs be called a proper faith? Can vegetarianism be a true religion? Can hedonism be a fervent stretch toward divinity? I think not, though, in those fragrant times, all these philosophical judgments, leaps of faith all, were made by students, however speciously and without a thorough debate led by our rationalist professors. After all, were not most students simply fueled by a simple hatred of Dead White Males? Given the jaundiced atmosphere of the place so far described, were not most students automatically inclined to see themselves as victims opposed by the same Dead White Males?

My point is this: Were we not all 'Cows, Cowed', both the mute students of which I was one and our professors who were afraid to lose their cushy jobs?

To pursue the metaphor a bit further down the grassy field, our laden udders were dragging upon the earth, our eyes were transfixed downward, and thus, we were completely unable to see the sky. We lacked all lucidity. Were we not depressed with fear and thereby daunted? Were we not intimidated by the unchecked enormous cultural forces armed against all normalcy? Was not the administration, at first afraid to lose, then disinclined to enter the fray with the extreme progressives? Were not most teachers understandably timid, browbeaten by these shrill forces of pseudo-religion, clothed as a healthy and vibrant irrationalism, that were marshaled by the immature and irrational students who preached against them? Who can now blame their tender quiescence, especially when one can look back and see how confusing and tragic those dim times were? Afraid to act overtly, carried along by fundamental changes in society's mores too quick and deep to fathom or to chart, some professors made themselves small, shrinking into the background, like extras at the back of the stage, and in time some became nearly as irrational and illogical as their recalcitrant and shrieking students.

Still, some rare teachers did not fall prey to these cultural changes. They remained resolute. Some, raised differently, still holding onto religion, its adhering vestigial tale left there by their parents, went back to being proper teachers; accordingly, they fought the good mental battles, pointing out the digressive idea, skewering the specious thought, transforming the poorly thought-out reading into a paradigm of lucidity. It seems now, of course, that complete bewilderment was nearly ubiquitous. Yet, this was a university, and presumably a top one, a place where clear thinking was supposed to be the norm. The norm! I now believe that, pushed by cultural forces too large to quantify, many professors, probably most, simply acquiesced. After all, they wanted to be liked, to be accepted as equals within the club, this poisoned academic milieu. And all claimed, or so they said with overflowing confidence, a surety of vision.

How is it that this fundamental transformation of thought has taken place? When, and more difficult to answer, how did this sharp and abrupt metamorphosis of a culture engender itself? I suppose (since it is only a guess, as I have learned now always to absolve myself in advance) it is only with simply the passage of time, and chance ruminations on old issues, the ones that will not depart, that can lend to one some new or fresh perspective. One may ask: Does harder maturity automatically make formerly fuzzy thoughts clear, or do they become clear only after much disciplined energy is applied to them?

Of course, the professors were not really in charge since the administrative leaders were, the over-paid and under-worked presidents and vice presidents. Most university leaders, even if privately repulsed or disgusted by drastic changes in the culture, lacked courage and will, and did little, not 'wanting to rock the boat'. Those leaders were inherently not likely to act and must have felt that they could not contest those two overwhelming forces: The sexual revolution and the drug culture, those two forces which acted like a brutal tidal wave upon our culture, and which, when stripped or pared down to their foul essence, essentially constituted an attack on Christianity, or, said another way, but one just as veracious, a new atheism. Abandoning their earlier charter of adherence to Christian traditions and since they did not want to anger the students, they simply acquiesced to them, gave in to them, which meant that they did not challenge the students, ask any tough question of them, or play the devil's advocate, but simply looked the other way, opening the door to all the massive social changes that we have witnessed over the past five decades.

Too, some of them did not want to fight, since they did not know how to fight, since, given their uniformly pampered lives, how would they know how to fight? Some of them probably became sullen, moody, or morose since they had been asked to work for a change. And most shirked that cruel duty and declined action, doing nothing but still cashing their biweekly pay checks. Their calculated passivity encouraged the growth of a diseased and sick society, one which embraces evil and vices, and where freedom and free speech, both already harmed by technology's sly algorithms, have been curtailed. During that fray, even while it was happening, I began to think that we were destroying ourselves, and that we had embraced decadence everywhere. Early on during my short two-year stint at the progressive academy, I had the overwhelming sense that evil was on the rise, that it is growing within our culture, daily ascending in strength and force, and that only with the strength that comes from prayer to God may it be surmounted and its rise within our culture curtailed. Here one may ask some simple questions: Are we still free people? What did we think was going to happen? Given all that has transpired, what values are today imparted at the university?

Then, to return to my close collegial stage, the world seemed to be an oyster. Everywhere only a world of ascending promise beckoned. Difficulties, illnesses, sufferings—all were never considered. Instead, the world appeared to be a happy place full of wonderful places to see, friendly people with whom to engage, simple thoughts without any scattered, raw edges to them: So, at the endless, presumably free parties, the obvious question was never asked: Who brought the beer?

Now, to me as a stark contrast, the world seems most tragic: People die, marriages fall apart, lawsuits become tyrannical, and many teenagers decline into drugs. This same place, this newly mongrel world to a viewer like me, it is a place older and tawdrier. I perceive it in a drastically different manner. How many of my fellow students still alive today understand with me that the world is an intrinsically sad place, one often full of suffering and distress, and that it is our job given to us by God, to be happy in it as a sort of metaphysical counterpoint, or as a paean to Him, a homage, while, temporarily, we walk upon it?

Finally, I ask myself: How was that conclusion, one which works, and one which is no longer tentative, ever reached?

* * *

As I look back upon those years, the students ran roughshod over the teachers, especially those who were not leading marches about Vietnam or advocating insurrection on the streets. All kinds of unconventional ideas were put out there, masquerading and quickly accepted as the bare truth: Homosexuality, drugs, Marxism, Eco-extremism, you name it. Those in power did not defend the rights of an individual, since he must instead be beholden to the greater rights of the state, or so it was preached. Slowly, incrementally, the rights of that individual, the very basis for our government, began to be demeaned, diminished. When a given professor did not immediately cave to whatever arcane, absurd, or patently ridiculous thought the students professed, he was squashed like a bug by the younger, screeching marauders. Political thought underwent overnight vast transformations, and for many proud elites in the discussion, the state became the ultimate authority. The individual, with his rights stemming from God, became subordinate. Overnight, and naturally, all commandments disappeared, evaporated, a little like an overnight mist does on a hot and steamy summer morning. These students mostly treated these teachers rudely and with disdain. Suddenly, unexpectedly, as a naïve 19-year-old, I was surrounded by very confident eighteen-year-olds who implied that PhDs from Oxford knew little. Consequently, many of the teachers became timorous and frightened. Today, at this composition, I wonder whether a teacher still may be called excellent when he is weak and not strong?

Sure, there were some teachers who pricked at hedonism's veil, who understood that life is meant to be full of suffering so that one may advance spiritually with God's grace achieved via prayer as an aid, and who knew that the supernatural is more real than this mean and temporary life. However, how could they fight against, argue, and expect to win such a huge cultural and spiritual battle? Oh, how the long odds were stacked heavily against them! These gigantic cultural forces against which all traditionalists were poised, which mocked all good done in the past, received little helpful criticism at the outset. How could the so-called progressives lose? Drugs, sex, whatever the issue … the mantra always was to go ahead, go ahead, do it. We will transform the world! Enjoy yourself! Release those inhibitions and do not restrain them! Never be such a fool! Impulse restraint is for idiots!

As one looks back today over those collegiate years, it is important to ask a key question: Were we not massively, collectively spoiled? Transfixed by a vivid array of false gods, we assumed that we always and preternaturally knew better: That cocaine would not harm, that free sex would help the family, that common ownership of all property hid no downside, and all the rest of the pap then proffered. All these ideas and dozens more were freakish assumptions dreamt up by disordered minds intent upon fundamental transformations of our society.

Also, the rampaging cultural majority held that so much of the past, its traditions of civility and decency, and especially, its religion, was bunk, worthless, and something to be quickly and thoughtlessly discarded like a worn tee-shirt that ends up in the garage or shop, there to be used as a rag to clean things up when the job is done. Did we even think to first put some of those hypotheses to a test not pre-judged? Or did we just quickly assume all of it to be true? God is dead, drugs are cool, sleep with whomever and all the rest of the predictable pabulum. The idea that is so sad, and so regretful, is that we did all this poisonous damage to ourselves; it was entirely self-inflicted and engendered by people.

Since we students had been told so many times that we were elite and special, or maybe because of a built-in arrogance, or both, we believed that we were special, an anointed generation, and that, since Evil does not exist, nothing bad would ever befall us. Since in those supposedly halcyon days all behavior was regarded as essentially equal, bad behavior could not exist, and therefore, it could not harm. Falsehoods and faulty propositions all! Please consider what devilish harm this unthinking acceptance and lack of skepticism have done to our culture!

No, not to put too damp a point on it: We were not special, nor close to it, though we thought ourselves so. And yes, we were that other 'S' word: Spoiled. And part of being spoiled means that you never say you are. I bet that many of our teachers were disgusted by us, disgusted at our illogical rejections, our specious reasonings, and our rude manners. At their lunches together, I can imagine my teachers Paul and George discussing the foolish certitude with which Student 'X' had announced that God was dead.

The student says this with the same blank certitude which he uses when he says,

"I am going to an acid party on Saturday night."

And both teachers then ask each other,

"How do you know that God is dead? Exactly how?"

I recall the two again: George, for whom I did paltry work, and Paul, when once in his class I did not read a text when I ought to have done so. I do not need to list their last names since, in the twilight of their years, they do not need the buffeting of my inflammatory castigations. They have put in their time. I can imagine this scene in the cafeteria. Between each other, in private at lunch over cottage cheese and melon, they would have explicated all our mistakes, pierced through all our assumptions, cautioned against all the untoward rejections. They would have said to each other away from the prying ears of the dictatorial, maniacal students,

"What the heck are we doing here?"

This is the same question all cynical soldiers ask as they prepare for an upcoming battle.

Yet, in the classroom, they would have much more reticent, and for this, I do not blame them. It is not my job to do so. In this polluted atmosphere where the First Amendment had been completely thrown over and discarded, they might have lost their jobs. Political correctness had just commenced! It was gaining much steam! And for the purposes of political persuasion and to bolster the powerful people in charge of things, free speech was already curtailed, truncated. Yes, it was. A student like me could no longer say what he believed without fear of reprisal or punishment or banishment. Yet, that is exactly how the freedom of the individual goes away, disappears, one word at a time. And guess what, I saw the whole thing happen! I was there! Fifty years ago, all these things happened right in front of my still-innocent eyes! I never knew better! Yet, one must ask, always: Is this the best that we can do, the very best?

Was I disappointed by this place? Of course, I was, for all the various sundry reasons just delineated, and, as I implausibly reach my golden years, I remain so. The over-paid administrators were acquiescent, lazy, and lacked moral courage. As Jim Bowie says about Colonel William Travis in The Alamo,

"I'd hate to say anything good about those long-winded jackanapeses." (Quotation taken from the film, The Alamo, directed by John Wayne from a screenplay by James Edward Grant.)

Simply put, no matter the mountains of hyperbolic and misleading praise that was heaped upon her, my alma mater was a diploma mill and a propaganda factory. Too, it is also a perfect example of universities and colleges in general, those that want to throttle dissent, freedom, and free speech, all of which means that, because of its fifty years of skewed politics and intolerant one-sidedness, we are in danger of losing Davy Crockett's revered Republic. Simply put: There was no candor there, no frank discussions, no searching for the eternal truth.

"The University of California at Santa Cruz Graduation: March 1973

A bachelor's degree in English Literature."

So reads my diploma, framed, which today hangs on the wall in my bedroom.

Four years earlier, in June of 1969, I had graduated from a rigorous Catholic high school, one run by razor-sharp Augustinian priests, a place where at that time and place free discussion was encouraged and open debate pursued, so, since that high school was my clear template of what an education ought to be, it was natural that I expected more from my university, much more. Perhaps given the perilous state of the university as I have here described it, which was more akin to a police state than anything else, I harbor little doubt that we are slowly and persistently destroying ourselves. The powers of government, presumably given to it from individual men, have only increased, because, asleep at the proverbial switch, we have allowed that government to seize those powers. I know one thing for certain: When the history of the decline of the United States of America is written years from now, front and center will be a discussion of how our once praiseworthy system of education was sabotaged and seized by progressive Marxists who played dumb, like the three blind mice, acting like they did not know exactly what they were doing.

I am reminded that in my hometown a long and serpentine assortment of variously shaped sandstone rocks lines the steep banks of San Antonio Creek. Occasionally, always when one least expects her to do so, often at night during an unexpected deluge, usually in the middle of winter but sometimes in the late fall or early spring, she overflows her banks in complete and surprising disregard for man's foolish intentions. Afterward, right next to her, people, even after all the mud, the incongruous debris of wooden posts, the bits of mangled wire, the dented and banged up mailboxes, the large white refrigerators, the worn and useless tractor tires, and the scraps of chain link fencing have been removed, they would decide to rebuild in exactly the same place, assuming that the flood of the surging San Antonio Creek would never take place again. And, soon enough, sometimes within one year or occasionally within five years, and surely within ten years, the monstrous watery disorder would return.

Uncle Francis

My memories of Uncle Francis are faint, but then again, aren't they all? Since I was then so young, only five when I first met him, I do not remember him well, and, when stoked by squinting memory, only the foggiest glimpses and snatches of tableaus come to mind. And I am sure, if he were alive today, that Uncle Francis would have only the vaguest and the least defined thoughts about my small and grinning face. So then, what is the point? To prove again, not that it needs to be again documented: Hoax memory creates the apocryphal, a bastard fiction. Memory is a cruel victim of our most larcenous intent, and, if it were a vehicle, it is a clapped-out buggy with bad wheels and no brakes, or as frail and pitiful as any once fierce old man on life-support might ever be. But, what the heck: One must try.

Francis was my father's uncle. When I first met him, I noticed that he had a very heavy beard, and the beginnings of what is termed 'a widow's peak' along his hairline. Auspiciously, he had been born on May Day, May 1, 1900, in the depth of the heartland, in Ashland, Wisconsin, a town situated at the extreme northern tip of the state overlooking Lake Superior. He would have been tall and barrel-chested, like so many of my Irish relatives were. He had the physique, especially the shoulders and torso, of an outside linebacker from a medium-sized Midwestern college. He had the small thick hands of one used to spending long hours digging in the stubborn dirt with a shovel. He was beyond healthy and, especially as a young man in his late teens, possessed considerable and surpassing speed. He had played a mean outside flanker on the football team in high school (he naturally disdained college as a place meant only for the idle and rich) and would run down the field after a vicious block, and then suddenly plant and pivot, plant and pivot. The guy could cut! He was an athlete unappreciated! Yes, his teeth were not great, a bit yellowed and crooked, but no one looked much at his teeth, but, instead, instead concentrated on the deeply set and blazing blue eyes above them.

Within our expanding Irish clan, there were plenty of Martins, Hickeys, O'Briens, and Dowlings among us. From birth, as a built-in destiny, all of us Irish figured that we had been anointed by God to be ministers or magistrates, that we were providentially in charge, that we ran the world and that it was our grand oyster. Therefore, it was verboten to marry outside the Celtic clan, at least for a few decades after our arrival in this country, straggling emigrants all, the tattered but feisty remnants of the Irish Potato Famine of 1845–1847. My dad used to joke and say to me confidentially,

"We are descended from a long line of Hickeys," but since I was still young, I did not then know exactly what he meant. My mom used to say that Uncle Francis looked a little like Gene Tunney, the Irish boxer, or the fighting Marine, take your pick. He had a wide and open face, a jutting jaw that seemed almost to be looking for a fight, and, again, those always flickering, lively, blue eyes, the blue the color of freedom and the deepest sea, gleaming, flickering blue eyes that would never tell anyone all that they knew.

Like so many young men back in the day, ostensibly wishing to set down roots or, else, feeling the fevered push toward carnality, Francis had married early, to be respectable, and, perhaps to tame or placate demon lust: Yet, who now can ever say such a thing, make such a jesting claim, with accuracy? It is surely not my job to hazard such an improvident guess. Velma was her name, a Jewish gal from a town near Ashland, and let me report as was once reported to me, trying, of course, not to embellish or distract in the process, that she was nobody to throw back! No sir! She was fragrant, feminine beyond normal range, and always smiling, that is, at least in those early years. She was not tall, perhaps through poor nutrition or childhood diseases (the flu epidemic had hit when she was still in high school, killing one of her little sisters), and as she gradually matured, her body seemed to swell or distend more than for some taller women. Still, it was her bountiful curves which had come so early to her, and it was her easy readiness to laugh at wry jokes or fleeting foolishness of any kind that drew him so irresistibly to her.

At first, together, they were top-dancers, woofers. That form of entertainment was quite popular in the twenties, and, wishing to expand on their possibilities, and perhaps tired of the long, snowy winters of Ashland, hard by the lake, Francis and Velma ventured west to Hollywood, that corrupt, luring, and irretrievably broken town where both the beauties and brawns yearn to be famous. For a full century it has been that seediest place full of illusions, phonies, and missteps, a charmless burgh full of con men, grifters, liars, and full-time unemployed cheats. Anybody who had been there some time quickly became unwittingly coarsened in one way or another, regardless of whether fortune had smiled on them or not. Yet, Francis and Velma had arrived like so many thousands of others from the Midwest, arriving at the train station in the early twenties, surprised by the heat, totting sleds, mufflers, and heavy overcoats, buoyed like thousands of others with teenagers' expectant glee.

However, once they arrived, they discovered, unfortunately, that the market for top dancers had disappeared, as if overnight. These things happen all the time in a town based on illusion, the merely fictional, and the importance of fads. Always, Hollywood cried out,

"It must be something new, anything new."

So, turning fast, acting like that once and always split end who knows how to run down the field, plant his foot left and pivot right, Francis, cutting fast, became a screenwriter and director for RKO and Republic Studios. During the twenties and thirties and into the early forties before the Japanese sneak attack on Pearl Harbor, Uncle Francis worked on dozens of projects, including silent films and the newly emerging talkies. Today I am sure that, using his buckets of Irish friendliness, endless charm, ready smile, and simple guile, he simply talked his way into those dozens of jobs. Uncle Francis was a scrambler! He worked on scripts for dozens of movies, frivolous entertainments then called shorts, banging those films into better, more finely honed shape, getting rid of the fat or esoteric, and always going for the bigger laugh. From his earliest days, as if gifted by God with gab, that pleasant gift arriving coincident with his birth, Uncle Francis was very good at getting laughs.

All this employ put him in close contact with the best and highest in the comedy world; therefore, he would have known or rubbed shoulders with other comedians including Buster Keaton, Charlie Chaplin, the Three Stooges, Laurel and Hardy, and who knows what lesser lights whose stars have dimmed more thoroughly from those gossamer days. As just a small sampling, he directed Cliff Bowes in Pep Up (1929), and W. C. Fields in Tillie and Gus (1933). As a writer, he would have crossed paths with Helen Twelvetrees in Disgraced (1933), George Burns and Gracie Allen in College Swing (1938), and Joe E. Brown in Big Mouth (1942). Too, for close to 25 years, Uncle Francis would have lunched at the studios' 'College of Cardinals', cafeterias to the stars ironically called that to point out their resolutely Jewish ownership. Even in the early days, those Jewish fellows were big on irony. At those famous lunchrooms, he might have met many other Irish actors of roughly the same age, whether they had been born in the Olde Sod or not: Pat O'Brien,

Edmond O'Brien, Brian Donleavy, one-eyed Raoul Walsh, James Cagney, Art Carney, William S. Hart, John Huston and his father, Walter, Tyrone Power, Bing Crosby, Ronald Reagan, Errol Flynn, Dan O'Herlihy, Dan Duryea, and Michael O'Shea to name just a smattering. And let us not forget O'Shea's wife, Virginia Mayo, and all the other Irish ladies of that era including Eileen Percy, Mayna Macgill, Patsy O'Leary, Mary Pickford, Helen Hayes, Maureen O'Sullivan, Geraldine Fitzgerald, and, of course, Maureen O'Hara. Oh, how the conversations must have soared, as Uncle Francis and his Irish buddies lunched on hot roast beef sandwiches or a Cobb salad, and coffee, lots of hot black coffee to better fuel the writers' imagination. Years later Uncle Francis would tell me with a straight face that Hollywood itself would not have come into existence if it weren't for the limitless mirthful talents of the Irish, with that heavenly gift sent to them by a smiling God. Too, whenever he was flush with cash, he would have dined at the elegant Musso and Frank's out there on Hollywood Boulevard, where the decadence had not yet reached its apex; and perhaps, I now imagine, one night William Faulkner, also fleeing his wife, might have mixed for him a mint julep, or told him quietly just how much shaved ice to add to his Kentucky bourbon. A man who enjoyed his drink, especially during the evening, to relax and plan for the next day, Uncle Francis would have drunk at least two of the cocktails.

Yes, Velma had been left out in the cold, put on ice, refrigerated. Francis' career put him in close contact with many producers and directors, and too, all their beautiful wives. Maybe the Navy vet, my great uncle Francis, had agreed with the Army vet, Ernie Pyle, who said that for any enlisted man it is always best to keep moving, to never stay too long in one place. Francis was inconsistent, unfaithful. He did not want to stay long in his marriage. There were so many other beautiful women, and irresistible temptations, everywhere! Everyone! Francis apparently thought some innocent, serial philandering would not have a deleterious effect upon his still-nascent career. Impossibly, crazed, perhaps he conjured that his career might even blossom with those carnal dalliances. Such is the strong prerogative of demon lust. Soon, Velma was completely out of the picture, so to speak, if the kind reader may forgive a faulty pun.

Predictably, given these trespassing inclinations, his career did not fully flower. Though he worked constantly throughout the 20s and 30s, he never reached that next, higher level of renumeration. Perhaps, to his credit, he did not wish to be famous or rich, knowing that most of them, the fancy elites, including himself, if he had been so chosen, deigned, quickly would have become just another patrician snob, full of useless scorn for all those plebeians of the hoi polloi beneath him. Instead, someone named Hitler intervened, and too, a violently macho fellow, former journalist named Mussolini added to the mix, and suddenly the once poor and pacified world of the Depression altered itself as if overnight to the stern uncompromising place of war.

Twenty-five years earlier, patriotic Francis, eager to fight in World War I, had lied about his age to enlist in the Navy. The pacifist-leaning President Wilson, late to war, had irritated him immensely. Like most Americans, in that first theater, he probably saw little action. Now, I wonder whether there is a record of his naval services somewhere, and can the big boys in charge, the brighter lights, ever find it? As it said in the Navy: There is always some SOB who does not get the word. I bet ten bucks that a secretary could not lay her hands on it no matter how hard she tried.

During World War II, Francis spent some of his time at the Navy Brig at Terminal Island in Long Beach. What must he have done? Given the lax, egregious standards of today, could his crime have been so awful to contemplate? Did he or his buddies pinch or sequester some whiskey? Did he stay out too late with some beautiful and fragrant woman? Did he tell some pompous ass, no-count Count, some do-nothing check-casher to cram it? So, what! The better point to make is that the United States Navy sure could have used some of the natural and aggressive inclinations of my relative, the Mick, in fighting the stalwart Boche or the renegade Nipponese.

One day (or so my father, his nephew, told me the story years later since indeed, I was not yet born when the following hilarious incident took place) toward the end of the second war, always sweet-talking Francis talked his way out of the brig. Of course, he did. Perhaps by behaving himself for a fortnight, he had merited a weekend pass, or, much more likely, maybe he had the goods, an inside scoop, on some dirt bag higher-up who had done something naughty or contrary to naval regulations.

So, outfitted in his regal dress blues, he went straight to his familiar haunts in his old-time Hollywood, that town full of seekers and suckers, the lost and the lonely. Somehow, he knew of a producer's house that was just then being sold; it was therefore vacant, and what's more, always clever Francis knew how to get into it. Once there, he called for dozens of his most vocal, meaning rowdy and outspoken, male friends, and scores of the most ravishing women, and I mean ravishing. They arrived, the men bringing cases of scotch, gin, and vodka, cartons of cigarettes (the ones advertising: L.S.M.F.T: 'Lucky Strikes Means Fine Tobacco', among them), and carloads of beer and wine. Too, they did not forget the bourbon. The party ensued and soon drew to it that most magic potion of any gathering of people intent on having fun: Ascending momentum.

Days passed. The boisterous party did not abate or slow. No doubt, away from the prying eyes of the street, there were many impromptu couplings in the back bedrooms. In those days, what with the war going on, people did not know whether they were going to live or die, so they lived each day and night as if it were their last. Soon, however, the Navy realized that Francis Martin was again absent without leave or AWOL, and it sent a small cadre from the military police (the MPs) to bring him back to the Long Beach Naval Air Station and the brig.

However, stalwart Francis was disinclined to such a proposition. He did not want to go there, so, astutely, he insisted that only the most enticing and comely of women, and many of them, deep cleavage bared, as if beckoning, to be there at the front door, with strong iced drinks already poured, when the MPs knocked upon it. To divert and confuse, the women suggested that the MPs might relax for a few moments with a chilled drinkypoo or two, probably in a foreign language, cooing,

"Pourquoi pas? Perce non? Por que no?"

Then, the splendid and beautiful greeters at the door would have escorted the MPs out to the second-floor terrace from whose height they might have viewed, between sips and grins, cuddles and winks, the somnolent and smoldering tall buildings of the center of the city not far to the east. From this point forward, the reader may embellish or insert, writing his own conclusion to the story.

Eventually, of course (much of this goes without saying), sometime later, a second small cache of MPs had to be sent out from Long Beach all the way 30 miles straight north to Hollywood to retrieve the seduced MPs and the always-grinning and wise-cracking Uncle Francis, now pleasantly and deliberately high on his favorite drink, which was scotch. It was no big surprise, my father later related to me that Uncle Francis was hauled back to the brig where he unpleasantly spent the few remaining days of the war.

I remember Uncle Francis most distinctly, from a time more than a decade later when I was approaching ten years, when fellow Irishman John Kennedy was president, and just after the Dodgers baseball club had arrived in town from the East Coast. Uncle Francis would show up at our house usually at noon on a Sunday with one gorgeous woman or another. He walked briskly from his car, and from the get-go, I could see that he was dressed nattily like some college English professor from New England, since for his whole life, even from tender childhood, as a 'born clothes horse', he had appreciated fine clothes. He was usually wearing grey flannel slacks, an oxford blue shirt, and a tweed or lambswool sport coat. If it were winter, his head would be topped with some sort of hat, either a fedora or an Irish wool flat cap, always worn at a rakish angle. Then, without wasting a second, he would start to crack them, one joke after another, like hot firecrackers all in a string. Uncle Francis was quick as anything, he had not lost one step in terms of delivery, and possessed an amazing, razor-sharp memory that worked smartly like a strong bear-trap. So, starting in without preamble, he would say, to anyone listening,

"I want to take my wife somewhere she's never been, someplace exotic. So, I say to her, 'Honey, here's the kitchen.'"

Or,

"What did Willie Shoemaker, the short jockey, say to the tall basketball player, Wilt Chamberlain?"

"I could have been tall too, but I turned it down!"

Or,

"I'll be taking my gal down to Tampa. Otherwise, Jacksonville."

Or,

"Three Jews on a train. What is this, a joke?"

Or,

"You know what happens when the government buys General Electric? It renames it General Candle, locks the doors, and shuts off the lights, that's what!"

Or,

"I thought that was my best joke. Heck, Marty, aren't you going to laugh?"

One time, in the middle of this Monte Rosa of funny one-liners, he looked at me, just a kid, and said to me all dead pan,

"It is good to be the king."

And then he said to me,

"We Irish narrowbacks run the world, bud, and don't you doubt it for a minute, customer."

And then he gave me a huge wink, which told me he did not really mean it. but that he was just playing around, fooling, joshing, and always full of beans or prunes.

My dad and I always got excited when Francis came around because he was so darn funny. The whole time he visited, it was just one joke after another. Hell, we did not even know where he lived. He'd just call and then show up, usually in his gorgeous 1951 burgundy 2-door Pontiac Chieftain De Luxe Convertible (the year with the red leather seats), walk in with some really luscious toot-tootsie babe on his arm whom my dad, fussing, cooing, and talking fondly, would adopt as his new, special friend, with she wearing a mink stole draped decorously over her naked shoulders, especially if it were winter. And then Uncle Francis would start telling the real howlers. One time I almost lost control and pissed up my pants, since he was going at a rapid-fire pace, telling jokes so fast.

However, truth be told, my mom did not like him so much. Not because the jokes were too racy (heck, after all she was a nurse and therefore used to some pretty rough material), but because every time Francis visited, he had a different woman at his side. It was never the same babe. I never remembered any of the gorgeous gals' names because, speaking only for myself, as just a kid, I was too busy drooling over each one of them, and for that good reason was way too distracted to remember a name.

After that, for many years we lost track of Uncle Francis, and then in 1965 we moved 90 miles northwest into the country and out of the city. During this time, I bet he took on many writing jobs where he was uncredited and got paid through back-channels. The last film he worked on was a flying saucer movie released in 1956. During this time my dad and Uncle Francis stayed in touch mainly by phone, since by this time Dad considered Uncle Francis, 14 years older than Dad, to be a second father to him. Somehow along the way, we inherited from him two love seats (please, no wise cracks, and weisenheimers, even today they are just in the next room) and some long guns (yet, they are long gone, but what I would give to have them here.).

Then, as always happens, many more years passed. One day, my dad got a call. Now in his seventies, suddenly and unexpectedly, Uncle Francis had moved out of seedy Hollywood. During that call, he said to Dad,

"Of course, it's corrupt. What did you think it'd be?"

And,

"I don't pay much attention to Wilcox. He is in show business!"

Francis had moved to southern Oregon where he met what was described as a 'young hippie woman' with whom he soon produced three young children. Had he finally understood that sex with too many women would kill the family as assuredly as the cat ate the canary? All that today is beyond my dreams. And, he also told Dad,

"I do not deal with Hollywood types anymore since it is too hard to separate the wheat from the chaff."

My dad and Uncle Francis had a long conversation with much loud laughing and guffaws at our end. You could tell how much my dad had missed Francis over the years, his hijinks sense of humor, his fun-loving nature, his near limitless capacity for booze, and his endless charm with all women, men, dogs, and cats, everybody.

Today I wonder: Did he find love with that hippie woman, or, what here during our fleeting time on this earth passes for it? Had he at last beat back demon lust or the mesmerizing pull of union? However, who am I to say?

And, today, I recall my mom that day saying to me with a warm smile on her face,

"For the longest time, he was one of those men who wandered, who constantly wandered, and who just could not settle. At least now, he finally did it, found a proper woman with whom to reside in peace for the remainder of the years on this earth that God will give him."

* * *

So, finally, now, after all these years separated by time and space, I understand how deeply, almost to the floor, my dad had bowed when he had heard that Lou Costello had died of a massive heart attack in his daughter's bedroom. Over the years, Lou's heart had been weakened by recurring bouts with rheumatic fever, a condition he had acquired in childhood. Per usual, his condition was much worse than anyone knew. As Lou bowed, as he fell, he clutched at her bedpost, but his grip was not strong enough. Lou was more or less gone as soon as he hit the floor.

My dad was so struck, so affected by this death or accident because Uncle Francis and Lou Costello had known each other. Right before the war, in 1940, they had worked together on a picture. I can't believe it is true, so I will say it again: Lou Costello, his partner, straight man Bud Abbott, and my uncle Francis had all known each other: He had worked with them on their first movie, called 'One Night in the Tropics', before the time in the brig, before the night of the MPs, before those ravishing women in the low-cut flowered dresses so popular of that time had beckoned. Why, I warrant, that they, the comedians and their wives had gone out to intimate little places downtown, maybe off of Lamar Avenue, which is not close to the ocean, slamming back watery and aldehydic Acme beer made just across the street and eating sweet platter loads of veal Marsala, and made with lots of mushrooms. These guys would have known on their own where to find the best veal in the city and they would not have needed any crooked Sally or corrupt police captain to tell them where to find it. They were just three fun-loving and laughing Irish guys eating Italian food. They didn't like fancy places with high prices, only good food, wholesome, served by only the most beautiful Italian waitresses, so you could wink at them, saying,

"Do you have any spinach. Holy mackerel! I said, Spinach, for all the requisite strength. Spinach. And oats. Oats!"

The jokes they must have told, ribald, racy, saucy, and thousands of them. One would lead to another, as surely as Sunday follows Saturday. People had more fun back then, that is for sure, and maybe that is the simple point of this simple story. The condescending, no-fun thought police have taken over, with their strait jackets and restricted reasoning. They are as much fun as cold toast. I imagine the three couples that night downtown on Lamar Avenue, eating the delicious veal and slamming back the beer. Today I imagine that maybe my folks went along too, to share in the lively, up-and-down laughter. Sad to say, my dad is not around anymore so I cannot ask him anything. If he were alive, thriving, quickly now, I would ask that of him, but in the meantime, which is now, I must assume that he also knew Lou Costello well and that all four of those Irish guys were all friends, chums, and buddies.

So, today I understand why my dad bowed so deeply when he heard the news of Lou's passing on. The date was May 3, 1959. I was a shrimp and only seven and one half. Sometimes, it takes a while to figure it all out. Maybe I am a bit slow like Uncle Francis, not regarding women, but slow otherwise. Maybe the Irish are slow, all of them which would include me. Sometimes it just takes some considerable time to piece it all together.

I know now that Uncle Francis stayed in the Grants Pass area along the Rogue River in southern Oregon for the remainder of his long life, not wishing to return to the rat's nest of Hollywood where, as he so aptly put it,

"It is hard to separate the wheat from the chaff."

During his many years in Hollywood working as a director and writer, Uncle Francis had made a ton of money and spent the same amount, if not slightly more. Uncle Francis died in Oregon's Josephine County on November 10, 1979, which meant that when he perished and left this temporary earth, he would have been living his eightieth year. I venture to guess that his wife and three children live on, with their fond memories of Uncle Francis intact.

I wish that I had asked Uncle Francis more questions, but, at first, I was way too young, and then later, when I had become naturally more curious and inquisitive, my great uncle Francis was way too old.

The veranda attached to the house overlooks the rust-colored canyon that leads up into the higher country where no one lives anymore. Mostly, we have abandoned the inhospitable outlying rocky reaches, those vermillion pastures that cannot make any money, or so we think. Always from this spot, on a clear day, after or whenever the Santa Ana winds had cleansed the sky, by looking the other way, southward, and usually with some squinting, one can spot the faintest suggestion of the sea at rest, the Pacific, which appears to be a shade of blue or grey, depending on the status of the sun.

Tonight, since it is summer and the days are long, a large party will gather there at the house. The prosperous revelers will spend the evening happily discussing recent home sales in the valley, what the current market conditions are, and what sharp uptick may be expected for tomorrow and for the fall.

Nonno Forzatore E Svanito: The Strong Grandfather Has Vanished

All of the Indians, especially those of the Chumash tribe that first inhabited these unspoiled territories, these bucolic plains and valleys, the uncluttered mesas, the dry-as-salt crackling arroyos and barrancas full of manzanita, toyon, and fir, all of it trying to ignite, to set itself on fire, once the season became even impossibly drier, well, they would have suggested to anyone within earshot that one should never speak unless one has something of good substance to say. The stern mien of the Chumash would command any man supposedly listening to them to fuller attention. And so, already, by these serious disagreements, lickety-split, our story begins.

First, they loved the outdoors and knew it. They could tell by the scent of the Matilija Creek which scrub was in flower, especially in the fall when the level of the stream was usually low and only barely gurgling, and the sumac, especially, was in bloom. Too, they knew enough not to build anything in the streambed, or anywhere near it, since one never knew when she, the mighty Matilija or the surprising San Antonio, or any of the many other rills whose lugubrious names are now mostly forgotten, might explode with water's fierceness and always unexpected and brutal force, surpassing and easily overflowing the pitiful sandy banks of the river. Instead, the Indians always built their small homes on bluffs or hillocks surrounded by trees which would provide shade for the dwelling: Eucalyptus, cottonwood, fir, or pine, and always with the simple dwelling's main bedroom inclined toward the East, towards the gaze of their own god who would look at them benignly whenever it is that they would try to grab some sleep.

That day, as I looked about, staring upriver a long way toward the sage-covered mountains, those whose herbal scent was all about me carried by the softest breezes, I could see that all the houses that used to line the Ventura River were gone. During the massive and unexpected floods of the winter of 1969, they had been buoyed down river, debris like flotsam and jetsam dashed, broken up, and scattered into balsa-like bits, pieces. Sometimes, looking down the river away from the mountains toward the opalescent sea, you could see bits of white, bright white: Refrigerators, I thought, jammed, pinned hard into some rock's crevice with an impossible force, when the storm had been at her vicious peak.

The Indians of all tribes never understood this lack of practical reverence for land. They never understood how California, once so grand, so untarnished, so pristine, had given herself so completely and fully to the mercantilist's endless push, meaning that she (for she was then still beautiful, unblemished, before her beauty had waned) would offer herself up to real estate's brokered rapacity, saying like some crazed or already surfeited lover,

"Take me! Take me again!"

And so, without surprise, she was taken. It took 50 years, which would be exactly equal to the life of three normally healthy dogs. Millions were made. Houses were flipped, and then flipped again, constantly, generating enormous profit. So many brokers, title officers, lawyers, and assessors were involved, those who had not done neither real work nor sweated, yet they licked their lips and clicked their teeth, for the bank accounts swelled, burgeoned to unanticipated and Gargantuan levels. Assumptions about what was right or proper were made endlessly, though they were mostly untenable, and would not work well over the long haul. Within this short lifetime, say, from 1950 to 2000, the state became over-mechanized, over-utilized, and despoiled. Water was stolen from lakes in the high mountains hundreds of miles away so that homeowners living in the impossible desert could water their lawns and wash their cars. Thousands of acres of enviable farmland (enviable to whom one wonders, since farmers have pretty much gone the way of the dodo bird, Sugar Hills, and disappearing paintings by Vermeer) were paved over with box stores, tract homes, gas stations, car lots selling new and used vehicles, department stores we do not need, and the ubiquitous Walmart, which are only erected to displace the smaller merchant and so that we can buy a candy bar for 85 cents instead of a dollar.

If we know and understand well and completely that real estate had run the state for all that time, we can also grasp that Hollywood's equally rapacious ethos had swallowed the valley whole, just like the shark that ate the marlin nearly as was written in 1954 by Ernest Hemingway, which was precisely when this gradual process of decline and disintegration was about to commence. For, unlike the Indians, we whites had little respect for the land.

So, towards the end of my senior year in high school, during the spring of 1969, and with me owning only seventeen years, the expanding and oh-so-groovy drug culture emerged, smacking the valley across the head with a vicious and sudden thrust. It was like a tidal wave or a vicious and unpredicted windstorm that topples trees and downs powerline, in a flash cutting off all power to the entire village. Brought in or procured by proud, black linen wearing Hollywood types, an array of drugs suddenly moved into the valley, though that introduction ought to have been foretold and expected; and that mind-turning inception was not a smattering: Jimsonweed, psilocybin, magic mushrooms, thousands of kilos of marijuana, and also pills of various sorts all promised nirvana, ecstasy, or a simple release or pardon from the common drudgeries of life. The introduction of the drug culture was entirely unquestioned and was immediately accepted as normal as a winter rainstorm or a hot day in mid-July.

At precisely the same time, as if on cue from some off-stage director, new and various physical promiscuities became common place. Also, acting as a joined-at-the-hip twin, people of the same sex began sleeping together, whether married or not, but not for a second longer than both wanted to, after which time a new, equally unhealthy shifting to another would be attempted or joined, until that new flame also lost its callow and temporary luster. The valley, which was my home only for my four high school years, became well-known for its high percentage of lesbians, and the more they moved in, the more they seemed to attract, like moths to a flickering flame, others of the same carnal ilk to follow. As if overnight, a new sort of Sappho cult was joined. This description is straight forward and simply an accurate recital of the facts as they transpired and came to life.

In summary, in the short period of years that encompassed my high school years, the town went from a hard-drinking, hard-screwing cow or agricultural town to a place full of fairies, fem butches, go-for-it gobbles, and bi-crossovers who were able to purchase all manner of illegal, mind-bending drugs. Quite abruptly, the old rules that had once ruled and governed the town had been tossed aside, like last week's tired salad. My high school town, which I still revered despite its new inclinations and bent, due to its low rates of rent (at that time, not now) became a famous destination for perennial loungers from throughout the west who might then gather there to live and lounge and not to work. The word was quickly circulated amongst 'street people' that the valley was a cool place to hang out, loll in doorways, smoke weed, and camp out, illegally squatting and trespassing down by the river. It had become the typical new sort of California town where you could no longer buy a round-point shovel or post hole digger but where you would have no trouble finding a piece of jewelry or bauble for your sweetie of either sex, since at that point fully twenty-six silversmiths beckoned. Yet, none of this I fully understood then, none.

Since all I knew then, as a teenager, near to college but still not shaving, was that people do not often listen to each other: No way in Sam Hell, as unlikely as a wench in church or a loose fart smelling pleasant to those around it. The rest of these meanderings would soon enough form themselves, but cast on whose anvil? Formed in what stove? They are dreamt of only in a manual yet one unwritten, told in a story only half-imagined whose words will not, up till the present, flow.

But, at that time, in those four short high school years, what I cared most about was running track. The rest was a bunch of drivel or downbeat dirge out of the future, which would be in a donkey's years. I was pretty good at track work, the mile and longer, plus the longer relays, since I then weighed less than a scrawny 150 pounds; and lately coach, since he needed someone else to do it, had asked me to have a try at the high hurdles, what he called using his Navy argot,

"The hubba-hubba hurdles."

And I told him I was going to try, with me thinking: Why not, pop? Why not?

My best friend on the track team that spring of my junior year was Alberto Torcollo, though, we called him Burt. He and his family, like many others, were busy shedding their Italian heritage as quickly as a teenage boy during summer tears off his tee-shirt before jumping into the river for a dip. We used to go on double dates together, and the four of us would yuck it up pretty good, convincingly, denouncing, spoofing, putting someone else down just for Jill's good sake, just trying to get the apprehensive girls to relax and then to giggle and laugh. It was all harmless fun really, and nothing spectacular happened one way or the other, though we did go through lots of gas. But, back then, Jasper or Butch, gas was cheap, around fifty centers a gallon if I can recall the number correctly.

That day in early June the Torcollo family was having a party, since it was his grandma's birthday, and Burt was kind to invite me. The family lived in a great house out on the east end of the valley. Their spread, grand, bucolic, and tidy, was something that Burt's strong grandfather, still very much alive, had bought and built, with his own gnarled and nicked hands, nearly by himself, brick by brick, board by board, using his old-fashioned perspiration, planning, effort, frugality, and sweat. None of the construction was easy. The expansive family house with quite high ceilings and large airy rooms rested on a 60-acre mostly flat parcel nearly entirely planted to Valencia oranges. They were very healthy, those trees, that much you could see while motoring in on the long cinder drive that was lined on both sides with pepper trees whose small red berries, once fallen onto the drive, crunched under the car's tires with small, popping noises. Today, as I write this, I can still see their unfallen red berries within the healthy trees which will shine in the sun, or glisten with moisture whenever it rains.

Then, that first Saturday in early June, I drove around a slow corner, and there it was: A large and gleaming white house (what some fellows might call a cape), one with a fresh coat of white paint and looking to me like it belonged back east, perhaps alongside the Providence River in Rhode Island. It had more than half a dozen bedrooms since there was no birth control available when the strong grandfather built her; furthermore, the Torcollo family did not have to be prodded, pressed, or sublimely coaxed to admit that they were firm, vigilant Catholics. Burt's mom, brown Sylvia, was beautiful and sultry in that sexy Italian way, with advanced curves in all the right places, and, of course, I secretly, impossibly, lusted after her, as was my steady job or periodic recreation. After all, a young man may dream, at little cost. From the first time I spied her early in my freshman year of high school, with her olive skin, dark brown eyes, and pleasing features, instantly she reminded me of the transfixing and well-known Italian starlets of the day, including, but not limited to, Gina Lollobrigida, Claudia Cardinale, Virna Lisi, Monica Vitti, Laura Antonelli, and the incomparable Sophia Loren. Yet, still, who am I forgetting? Anna Magnani for one, doofus. From those early days, thinking quickly, I knew in my heart that I needed to find someone much younger than Sylvia, much younger, plus someone not already married to somebody else, which would be Burt's dad. All through the four years of high school, I never told Burt about this unrequited, and un-acted upon desire or hankering since I knew that Burt, or any one of his many brothers, would have popped me right away with a hard punch to the chin if I had.

Scattered around the ranch that day, and surely too to this day, so long do they last, better than people, healthier than folktales, were oak trees: Huge ones of a darker, pentland green, four or five or six stories high and equally as wide. Grandpa Torcollo never removed any of the oak trees before he planted the Valencia orange orchard or built board-by-board the large and gleaming ranch house, since, as he said,

"Kids, those oak trees, they were here long before we were."

We were there that June day for Nonna's party, Grandma's party, which to me was the high point of early summer, that is, if social stuff was important. The Torcollos had brought in dozens of bales of hay that people could sit on or roll upon. Some of the bales' wires were cut with wire cutters, and the straw had been spread about evenly under the oak trees and eucalyptus to quell the rise of dust. All sorts of fruits, especially watermelon and cantaloupes, were halved and iced. Large aluminum tubs were filled with root beer, cream soda, and lemonade, all nicely iced to the point of being almost frozen. There were drinks so cold that whenever you drank one taken from down deep in the bucket, the liquid would for a few long minutes hurt your throat and tummy all the way down, until after a while, like most things in life, the pain went away.

The best event of the day was the slow roasting of a goat, a kid goat: La capra, il capro; a nanny goat and a billy goat. The slow roasting, started with split oak wedges, required many hours, with the fire started early the day before, with the burn pit having been dug deeply into the earth; the animal, swabbed with garlic, soy, and rosemary was then wrapped in several layers of wet muslin and cheesecloth. It was roasted slowly like that, slowly through the night; and then roasted some more during the next day, today, and only six hours earlier the oak fire had been re-stoked with more oak wedges but slowly so. And a whole lamb, unexpectedly arriving from a distant cousin had been added to the slow roasting as well.

Grandpa Torcollo, whose first name was Bartolomeo, laughed loudly when we told him, I listening to him closely, as all jesting and teasing teenagers must, that he had a long first name, one with a whopping five syllables. He said to me,

"Che? What? Have you ever heard of my brother, Ermenegildo or il mio cugino, my cousin, Ludovico? Can you imagine having a name like Ludovico

Torcollo? Why, just to say the name takes longer than washing the car or doing the laundry. Eventually my mother got tired of all the syllables so the three little ones, my younger siblings, are Edoardo (spelled with an 'o', mind you, mio pazzo e rocca), Ana, and her later brother Aldo. Alora. Dopo. Avanti. Like the cigar. Soon we must all go forward. To eat. It is close to time. To eat! Mangiate!"

Grandpa Torcollo, the strong grandfather, Nonno Forzatore, as many frequently called him, with his long name sometimes shortened to "N.F.", always made the call on that June Day as to when we would begin to eat. Annually, on the first Saturday in June, I came to understand, it was his happy job to make that precise determination, and he gloried in such small patriarchal powers. Every year he would choose the exact minute to commence the long feasting. Even though the tantalizing garlicky smells of well-roasted goat and lamb filled the summer air, suffusing it with those hunger-feeding scents for hours, old N.F. would not be rushed, since as he said,

"The meat, it must be falling off the bone."

The whole Torcollo orange ranch smelled like rosemary and lemons, olive oil and fennel, sage and red wine, and garlic and cilantro. Finally, after having foolishly filled my stomach with too many root beers and bits of melon, after Burt and I had been telling the same lame stories at least 3 times, and after I had been blindly peering at Lucinda's (one of the Torcollo's more comely daughters) charming backside at least four times ("Quattro!" She yelled at me, "Quattro!" and me, the dope, thinking she just wanted me to give her a quarter), that is when I heard N.F. yell proudly to the crowd in that deep, grizzled, grappa-and-amaro laced voice of his, his unshaven paisano face festooned with soot, grease, and spittle, his chapped lips laced with dirt and red wine,

"Il tempo a mangiare. It is time to eat now, please. Adesso! Al tavolo! To the table! Please! Prego!"

But, of course, as a garrulous Italian, old N.F. then got a bit sidetracked. Someone had mentioned the word 'death' and the phrase 'ball in chain' in the same sentence, and his dark brown Italian eyes (Yes, they were the exactly that same color as the fine, slightly bitter amaro made by Meletti from Ascoli Piceno in the Marches) lit up, and in a theater manager's loud voice, he explained his situation to the crowd,

"My cousin, Ludovico, he still lives over there. Ancona. Ancora. I made a small joke. Can you imagine having a name like Ludovico? It sounds like a stiff cat falling down the stairs. Ha! Anyways, Ludo, as we call him, cannot stay married. No. My friends, it is not that he is unfaithful. No. It is that his wives, they keep dying on him, four of them, right in a row. Let me recall for you their various names,

Renata

Adrianna

Sophia

Lucia.

Old Ludo! You must understand that by this time he had become tired of dealing with this problem of his wives dying on him, one from a stroke, another from runaway downstairs female problems, the last two from some other sort of fast-acting cancer, so he says to himself: I will get myself a young one, really young, the better to avoid the man with the scythe! So, not long or much later, he found himself a ripe tomato, a real peach, a terrifically attractive one, a brunette with an expressive and bold femininity named Yolanda! Naturally, or perhaps not, his various children from his various wives (indeed, enough wives, five, to field just by themselves a basketball team) were put off, repulsed, nearly disgusted, at what they deemed to be his licentious behavior. Some thought he was too lecherous. Can such a conclusion be true? Others deemed the new one,

'La Bella Numero Cinque'

as Ludo called her, or

'The Beautiful Number Five' to be a gold-digger, a welsher. But, not to my brother! He was no sweet pea, or someone easily duped. So, with a Torcollo leer in his eye, with no strain or pull on his face, calm and tranquil, he says to his mildly complaining daughters, "Not to worry. I will outlive her too. I figure it this way: If she dies, she dies, and immediately I will look for number six."

"You have to watch the pronunciation there. Stai Attenti! Careful! But enough talk. Basta! Enough! Let us eat! Mangiate! Mangiamo! Mangia bene, caca forte, evita la Madre della Morte! For, let us now recall the well-known phrase: Eat well, shit hard, and avoid the Mother of Death. Preghiamo! Let us pray!"

And with that, my best friend's strong grandpa, Mister N.F., said the Italian grace before meals in a loud and commanding voice so that all attendees gathered at the dozen picnic tables at the grand June party could hear it. Then, he strode over to the serving table full of cooked dead animals: Goat, lamb, some beef, and chicken. With a long knife, one of proper tempered steel and that had clearly been passed down to him through the ages, he began to slice and carve the loins, flanks, breasts, and thighs of meat, to offer watching and passing picnickers their pleasure and choice. I could see, as I watched and studied him that day, now so long ago, that Nonno Forzatore, Mister N.F., looked like he couldn't be happier. He said to himself as he loaded up the plates,

"We must do all of this and more, and quickly so, now, hubba-hubba, chop-chop, presto, adesso!"

He smiled often, especially at all the women, when his eyes would instantly twinkle and gleam. To the men, he made frequent grunts, derisive catcalls, and scuttle-butt guffaws. In a word, that day he seemed like a king, so grand was his palace and so spontaneous his mirth. His brown Italian eyes told me,

"Let mirth become a feast. Let us always make and then keep and guard a feast of mirth."

So, that is it, the gist of the story. I didn't find a girl's heart that day, and not for want of trying; and nor did I get to sneak away to down any Hamm's or Schlitz or Blatz lager and thereby become under the hot afternoon June sun gently mottled, sozzled, or juiced. However, as I left slowly in my truck, I did see an older couple playing tonsil hockey, necking like crazy on the far edge of the grounds, out past the last pepper tree of the drive just before the first trees of the orchard. I did not know who the hell they were, nor did I give a rat's fart or ransom. I figured they both were out on the prowl with each other, terrifically horned up, and obviously angling for some out-of-line, impromptu nookie. Was she a blowen? He a crotch hound? Anyway, it was not up to me to judge or rank their rookie carnal misdemeanors. They were going at it like drunk teenagers, copping feels, and getting frisky. I think I scared them a little or a lot, since their glances back to me were fox-quick and furtive. Then I heard from both lovers, as I slowly drove off and as they scurried away, like a crab might race across the ocean's floor, high, clear, and ascending giggles.

* * *

That next year, still girlfriend-less, riddled on my teenage face with what my less kind classmates called,

116

"Nick's infinite red volcanos," I went out for the track team. The coach in my final track season assigned me to the mile, the two mile, the longer relays, and even though I possessed little real speed for the sprints, the 110-yard-high hurdles. I was little more than a fill-in, really, just a body, so that the team might earn a few extra points in the scoring. The 'real' hurdler was Richard Connors. He had an athlete's physique, lightning speed, and coordination well beyond mine.

When he first saw my ridiculous attempts, he just looked down at the ground. And his disconsolate attitude summed it up: Second fiddle, too heavy, an in-and-outer, terrible.

But, gently, over the course of that long season, all through the months of February, March, April, and May, and showing great patience, he tried to coach me. As I said before, since people do not often listen to each other, and as I did listen closely enough to his coaching, it didn't work. I can still recall the irritated, disgusted look in his eyes (since he had given me these same directions many times before) with him saying,

"Listen, Nick. After you pass or skim over the first hurdle, right afterward, you must snap that lead leg down fast, hard, so you can start running again. Do you hear me?"

Maybe I was listening to Richard, but not hard enough, not concentrating enough on his words. Anyways, I just wasn't as good as he was, and did not possess his inordinate natural talent for the high hurdles, that's for darn sure.

My best friend, Burt, was a little on the chubby side, what they used to and still call 'oversized' or 'chunky'; therefore, he put the shot. At practice, we hardly ever saw each other, so it was only on the meet days, when we would take long, slow, bumpy bus trips to Santa Barbara, Santa Inez, Carpentaria, Newberry Park, and sometimes heading north to Santa Maria, that we would huddle together at the back of the bouncing bus and tell long meandering stories to each other, sure groaners, or the smallest of lies, making up the lamest jabs, foolish joists, or tallest tales.

Unexpectedly, his mom, Sylvia, had contracted multiple sclerosis, in the last year. The disease had come on strong, that was starting to wear on him, since it hurt him to see his own mom suffer so thoroughly. No medicine or antidote could be found to deter the savage march of the disease upon his mother, so that there was nothing he or anybody else could do to help her, besides saying constant prayers, that she would be calm and not in pain.

One day, that spring, I remember us sitting in Father Taube's Religion class, as the priest said to us,

"Only suffering, sometimes entering quietly as a dove, compels spiritual progress."

I happened to glance over to Burt just then and saw in the comer of his eye the smallest tear which he immediately dabbed at with the sleeve of his coat.

* * *

Years passed. I went away to college and then took various summer jobs, as one does. In the meantime, the 'recreational' drugs had firmly taken over the valley and our culture as a whole in a sure-handed, methodical way so that we might more quickly destroy ourselves from within. Too, sex took on an inordinate role in our culture and served to near-kill the family, reminding me again of the happy cat that ate the canary. And, more and more, society coarsened beyond all description and reason. Finally, selfishness abounded, so that, rather than people caring a rat's ass for others, aiding and helping others, we fought only for our own, mostly private gain.

The Torcollo family, though, mostly stayed together and supported each other through all these changes, all these travails, all these mockeries. For some years, I lost track of Alberto, my good friend from high school, but then one year, somehow, with both of us home at Christmas from college, we reconnected and went out to a local watering hole for a few beers, to chew the fat, to tell some old lies to each other, and to go over old times. Immediately, we kidded some, as old buds do. So, out of the blue, he says to me,

"You were always crap in the high hurdles. You did the 4-sttep, not the 3. Don't you understand that you can't win jack or diddly with the 4-step, Nicky? Snap the lead leg down! It had to be the hubba-hubba hurdles all the frigging time."

And so, I said to him,

"Give it a rest, will you? Please. Burt, I have heard all of this before, from Connors, during that last spring. I know I was lousy as anything!"

We talked about all kinds of things. Old friends always have many things to talk about: Girls, cars, sports, and girls, girls, girls; and so, after we covered that exhausting subject and we were both tired, I asked him,

118

"How is the old Torcollo place in the East End, that solidly built ranch owned by Nonno and Nonna? How is it? I assume that it is just as grand, bucolic, and tidy as ever."

And Burt said, to my enormous shock and surprise,

"Grandpa Torcollo, old Nonno Forzatore, had a sudden, massive heart attack and died, and with that painful event in place, his vision disappeared, evaporated, vanished. Svanito! Svanito! Nonno Forzatore E Svanito. The strong grandfather has vanished, disappeared. It is clear that we do not make men like him anymore. That is to say that with him dead, the place just fell apart. Gone. It is gone, and in no time at all. Nonna is still around, but she is just a vestige of her prior self, a mere shell. It all happened very quickly, before many people realized what the heck was happening. It did not help things to have such high taxes, and too, some of my dad's siblings suddenly became sissies, ninnies, complainers, schlubs, nitwits, call them what you will. They were no longer willing to work hard there, to carry out and complete the long and dirty farm work that pretty much no one wants to do anymore. Nicky, somehow a ubiquitous laziness crept into our once-strong family and settled down there to make itself comfortable And, then finally, you have all the other lounging idiots of that once-resolute family making lame, weak, and meek excuses, like complaining about how the high labor and water bills were eating us alive. After all of that, the ranch was sold at too low a price, not that anyone ever asked me. Think of all the work old Nonno Forzatore, Grandpa Torcollo, put into the place, and grandma Nonna as well who did more than her share, and now the Italian hacienda is owned by some cheesy-ass Hollywood producer. Of course, it is. Nicky, I bet you ten bucks that the new opportunistic lunkhead owner wears black linen only and probably makes dirty movies to sell to kids, to warp and to irretrievably harm those young minds. Let him. I try not to think of the old place much anymore. After Grandpa died, the whole thing went to pieces, and all of this happened, seemed to take place in less than a minute. It all makes me wonder: Have Americans forgotten what work is? Nonno Forzatore had come to this country from the Abruzzi as a teenager fifty odd years ago and worked hard, and now in two generations everything he worked for is gone. I am sure you understand, Nicky, that every family, every empire crumbles, caves in on itself or destroys itself from within, not without. And that is what happened with my family, the Torcollos."

I was saddened too by the story, maybe more than Burt. I asked myself: Didn't the next generation realize that they would have to work hard to keep it, and maybe sweat a little?

But then, and quickly, I answered my own question with a bit of Navy wisdom that I had somehow over the years picked up from my dad who had been a Navy man during the war, thinking that there is always some son of a bitch who does not get the word.

I thought how the strong grandfather always looked so strong and vibrant. But perhaps his arteries and veins were blocked, plugged, occluded. Maybe the walls of his heart muscle were made thin by N.F. drinking too much amaro and grappa over the years. And after all, Nonno was 75 years old and nobody lives forever, right?

Pensively, Burt and I finished our last beers and said goodbye to each other, vowing to not give each other a wide berth in the future, but, instead, with both of us realizing that friendship is very important, we made firm plans to see each other again next Christmas.

Achtung, bitter: Attention, please.

Our get-up-and-go got up and went: Away, that is. Nine times out of ten, nowadays, our leaders do not measure up, nor are they close to doing so. They are wastrels all in a muddle. When confronted with a problem, they circle the wagons, to protect their fellow, lazy brethren; and then they vote for the formation of a task force, done to retard any sense of responsibility and so that they may more easily stew and fester, both of which means to do nothing. They are foggy phantoms, Hollywood numb-heads, who do not own the goods or gumption to get much done. Unfortunately, they have taken over our culture and government, these do-nothing mavens and excuse-making magistrates. Sometimes these folks have their own agenda: To raise the state and belittle the common man. We no longer know how to lead since we grew up never following an order. So, Foxhole Normans are everywhere, those who do not know how to fight. We are surrounded by so-called men who are nine-day wonders, who are akin to flash fires made of straw, 'Il Fuoco di Paglia'. A straw fire is one that burns quickly and brightly but does not get much done, nor produce much lasting heat.

Meanwhile, many of them have also grown a chip on their shoulders more quickly than pancreatic cancer metastasizes. They are inclined to be lazy and self-serving, and quite likely to play the victim. Our government promotes decadence which in turn is dooming us. Does this not mean that there is a deep and ever-deepening corruption at the heart of the American Dream? Most empires crumble and fall; or is it truer to say that all do so? We are governed by a class of ruling elites who do not rule and are not elite. Perhaps we need to think of a good dentist who sees and quickly identifies a bad tooth: He knows well that, sooner or later, that bad tooth shall have to be pulled out completely, and by the root.

The Slightest of Stories

A long time ago, before I was even driving, just before the start of our basketball games, I would go up to the half-court line and chat up the opposition, not to intimidate them, but, as one recalls now, I must have been lost in some sort of nostalgia for comradeship, that is, to operate in a friendly style with complete strangers. Was I full of untoward and unwarranted friendliness? Coach Ferrari probably thought so, yet he said to me little on the issue. So, on a given day so many seasons ago, I would say to this player from Oxnard on the opposing team,

"What do you think of our gym? It is unique and offers tons of character. It is a clear classic. Pretty neat, don't you think?"

The truth was the place was a simple brick building with little heat, many dead spots on the maple floor, very little room beyond the out-of-bounds line before you hit the mostly unpadded brick wall, and on and on. Built as the first gymnasium in the valley, constructed during the 20s, it had not been maintained well and was really showing its age, especially when compared to the fancy new gyms of the public schools that had recently appeared all over the county. It was long before I figured out that those new gyms were paid for by always-rising property taxes, since if a guy owned a decent place, it would likely cost him ten thousand dollars to sleep in his own bed. So much for the once solid American dream of home ownership! Years ago, that dream went out the window or flew the coop, killed by the following quintet of lazy sharks: Realtors, school district administrators, bankers, appraisers, and assessors.

The short point guard from Oxnard was astonished. He said to me,

"You're nuts! This place is a dump. You've probably never even seen a decent gym!"

I had, but I didn't want to let him know it. Was this one-upmanship? Psychological tricks and games? And so, I said to him,

"We think it's pretty cool," and went back to my pregame drills.

Believe it or not, we won that game. Not long afterward, when the green grass of California winter (that being a near-drought year) was already on the cusp of turning to yellow-green and then gold, we traveled by lopsided bus, one with lousy shocks, to their digs down in the old La Colonia section of Oxnard.

And, to do so, Brother Bill, our bus driver, drove through the Santa Clara Valley at 45 miles per hour, passing tractor sheds, tidy farms growing vegetables and some citrus orchards, mostly lemons, shining bright yellow in the warm winter sun. On the edge of the small towns, though, you could already see the suburban spread pushing inevitably its way onto the rich farmland. Dirt, rich black alluvial soil 30 feet deep, perfect for growing just about anything, was about to be covered over by box stores, tract homes, car lots, you name it. Those favoring pretty much all developments were, even then, packing the city councils and planning boards and land commissions so that the real estate interests would always get their way, always. This is the smug, predictable and rapacious story of California and much of the West. And this path is a one-way street since once good farmland is covered over by commercial or residential leapfrog development, that land shall never be farmed again. America does not well protect our land since the pull of greed, the desire to get rich by doing precious little, is so strong and unremitting.

Smelling the shrimp tacos, corn tortillas, chile verde, and refried beans emanating from La Colonia's dozens of Mexican restaurants, our creaky bus pulled into Oxnard, found the fancy public school gym, where we changed our clothes, getting into our stinky, rarely washed basketball uniforms. In the locker room Coach Ferrari, using his hands like a boxer punching the air, delivered his usual loud, demanding, and repetitive speech about teamwork, defense, effort, and all the rest of that stuff we had heard from him at least one hundred times. At the game's start, I warmed the pine, which was probably the best place for me, since there I would accomplish the smallest amount of damage both to myself and the team.

The game was one of those ugly see-saw jobs where nobody could hit a lick and everyone was making stupid fouls and turning the ball over, and it was so bad that it was almost as if you got points for lousing up, making a mess of things. And then suddenly, out of the blue, as happens sometimes, our wingman and by far our best basketball player, David Collins, began to get hot, hitting long shots from the corner, the top of the key, everywhere, one after another. Improbably, we took an 8-point lead halfway through the 3rd quarter, things looked pretty good, and I thought to myself, while still riding the pine: *Perhaps we shall get a win in Oxnard's La Colonia. Perhaps.*

However, Coach Ferrari was not happy. Truth be told: He was rarely happy. His dark brown eyes told the entire story: No, sir. He did not care for the gunner mentality that he observed in Collins' play. He wanted the scoring to be well distributed among the entire team. He called for a time-out and spoke to Collins directly, saying,

"Look! I don't want you shooting anymore from the outside, get it? This is a team game, and we work for the lay-up. Pass! Pass! I want to see five passes in a row before anybody takes a shot, do you hear me, gentlemen? And Mr. Collins, if you take another shot from the outside for the rest of the 3rd quarter, even if you're wide open, you're benched for the game's duration. Do you clearly understand me?"

Collins said,

"Sure, Coach. I get it. No problem."

The game resumed. Sure as shooting (and please excuse the pun), on the next play down at our basket, Collins, ball in hand after a deft crosscourt pass, was again left completely open. For a tick, he must have forgotten what Coach had just said, and then, as he prepared to take the 20-footer, his feet already having left the maple floor, he remembered coach's clear command. The result was a predictable failure: An air ball, a weak floater, a dead duck!

As soon as he could, Coach Ferrari called for a time-out and benched Collins. Coach didn't say much, and I could see that he was fuming, pissed off, about to go bonkers. We ended up, of course, absent our best player, getting shelled, laced, hosed. Our clock was cleaned. And so goes the endless struggle, Nelson.

But, afterwards, on the long bus ride home, Coach Ferrari was no longer angry. After all, he had taught us a lesson, that teamwork was more important than individual scoring, that good teamwork would lead to unity, and that good unity would lead to that rarest of things, that most elusive of human charms, unified success. By benching Collins, who had done nothing wrong, Coach Ferrari had shown to us, offered, the goal of what constitutes true teamwork, and, by extension to the greater world, how all the components ought to operate on any team: They ought to mesh seamlessly. From that point in the season onward we would play like a joyous band of brothers, and because of that subtle improvement in play, for the first time in many years, remarkably, unexpectedly, we began to win more basketball games than we lost.

That distant night lost in the passage of time, we began to feel some of that special feeling of camaraderie on the long, slow, bouncy ride back home. Most of us were clustered in the back of the tilting bus, gathered there telling slightly racy stories, trying to impress each other that we were worldly and manly, when we were clearly not.

Once, in the middle of listening to Fitzmaurice tell, for the ninth time, the long goofy story about the guy who has been on a desert island for years and the beautiful, tanned woman wearing a tight, zippered wet suit, carrying a set of golf clubs, who suddenly walks out of the sea, and who says to the man on the desert island,

"Do you want to play around?" Laughing at the silly joke, I looked up and saw Ferrari's face and his dark brown eyes. He was at the front of the bus, using his typical emphatic gestures inherited from his totally Italian lineage, telling something important to Brother Bill. His eyes told me that he was happy and that even though we had lost the game, in truth we had won it. We had won the bigger battle, that battle for our souls, though, of course, we did not realize it at the time.

Because of the way the game had gone, it had afforded Coach Ferrari an opportunity to teach us a lesson. As a sharp and inventive coach and teacher, he did not want to miss that chance to guide, that opportunity to instruct. Even today, down through all the intervening years, across the expansive span of both time and territory, I can still remember his smile and that lively sparkle in his dark brown eyes.

"Farthest from your mind is the thought of falling back, in fact, it isn't there at all. And so, you dig your hole carefully and deep, and wait."

The quote is taken from the 'Currahee' Scrapbook of the 506 Parachute Infantry Regiment from the 101st Airborne and the 2001 film Band of Brothers, created by Tome Hanks and Steven Spielberg, and based on the 1992 Stephen E. Ambrose book of the same name.

According to legend, 'Currrahee' is the Cherokee word for 'Stands alone'.

Whose War? What King?

—I'll stay. I'll watch. I'll guard.

—Wait a moment. Someone has to get going or pick it up.

—Zauber, the German word for magic. Today we need some of it. We have annoyed and therefore trifled with all the gods. And for that reason, they are not happy with us.

Therefore, friends, we will need prayer and action, and not a little zauber. But, first, prayer is required, as a catalyst and to get things going. So, friends, let us pray. Sic populi oremus.

Shall we sail a boat, sailor, sail a boat upon the churning sea?

It was mid-July of 1960, once again I am eight years old, so we are back at the very beginning, thereby making bookends. Democrat Jack Kennedy, 100% Irish by blood, had been sunning his famous face, and more, somewhere. Was it over at Marion Davies' luxurious home on Beverly Drive in Beverly Hills and near to the Los Angeles Sports Arena where, soon enough, he would accept his party's highest nomination? The nation's highest office: The Presidency? Did he really hop a fence or gate to get there? Whose fence? What gate?

Some weeks passed. On the way to the New York studio for their first debate, his Republican opponent, Richard Nixon, had banged his bony kneecap, the patella, hard against the doorjamb of a yellow taxicab. Blazes! Crap! That is what happens when a fellow is distracted and not paying proper attention to the moment: Bad things, coming out of the blue, can quite easily happen. This was no darn joke and for Nixon, the injury smarted and hurt like heck. Too, the Republican candidate for many days had been fighting a nasty flu bug with antibiotics; however, nevertheless, the virus had refused to go away. So, when he entered the building and first spied his handsome and strapping nemesis, it must have been, we can now imagine and attest, quite a startling contrast: Nixon, in pain, looked sweaty, ashen, haggard, and seriously in need of a close shave, and Kennedy appeared fit, relaxed, smiling. Nowadays it is provident to ask a pesky question from the mists of history: Had the famous Irish American just been with a woman, perhaps to more easily relax, to sooth his tensions, before the crucial debate? For many of those who only listened to the debate on the radio (those who only listened to the debate were still common throughout the land then since we had not yet sacrificed ourselves before the television, like lambs or common goats might have done, prostrate in front of the latest technological god), they concluded that Nixon had won handily. But to those, most that is, who watched it on the small, black-and-white televisions of the day, grainy, irresolute, Kennedy, gracious, smiling, and deft, was clearly the champion.

The next night at dinner, I asked my dad,

"What does it take to be your winner, Dad. We're Irish Catholics, like Kennedy, so I don't understand why you're not voting for him."

I was not yet 9 years old, so how much real water could be in the well? Dad looked at me closely, and his eyes narrowed a bit, like they always did when he was advancing a point. He cleared his throat and said to me,

"Kennedy is only an upstart, someone unlisted. His daddy, Joe, is paying for everything and more. Too, I've heard it alleged around town that your man, Jack, is a complete horn-dog or crotch hound. So, I ask of you, son: Do we need that trait in our president? And I do not believe that he has enough leadership experience to be our commander in chief."

Quickly, I asked him,

"What about PT 109? Didn't that incident show considerable leadership on his part?"

Just as swiftly, my dad countered,

"Let's talk about something else, son. I'm tired tonight. How are you hitting the ball? What about curves? Okay? Better? Remember, son, that you must wait a little when trying to hit a curveball. You must darn near snatch it out of the catcher's glove. And then smack it to rightfield. Do you hear me, to rightfield?"

Unfortunately, the truth was this: My hitting was getting worse, always getting worse.

Some time passed. Back then, I only cared about baseball, how the Dodgers were doing (they had arrived in town not too long ago, just after my 6th birthday, and in just their second year they won the gonfalon, the pennant.), what position the coach had me stationed at in Little League, and how I was hitting the white bean or nugget. And that meant: Forget girls; just forget them. I told myself more than once, since I already knew that they were a waste of time, completely.

Anyway, lately, the only hitting I could manage was a few slow grounders or weak Texas Leaguers that barely floated over the infielders' heads. I used to keep track of my batting average; however, now, after some months that spring of 1963 (Yes, Kennedy had won the whole shebang two and a half years earlier, yet there was frequent talk, talk that would persist and not go away, my dad told me, of dead people voting in Cook County, Illinois. However, I wondered: How could that be? How could dead people vote?) it, my batting average, was so low that I stopped making the calculations in my head. I said to myself: Why bother? Since, if it goes below .275, all bragging rights are lost, kaput, and Gonski.

Sure, I was decent in the field catching looping fly balls or snagging nasty, short-hop grounders, but who the heck ever talks about someone being a good fielder unless you're the Dodgers' shortstop, Pee Wee Maury Wills or someone like that, maybe his teammate Willie Davis, for example, or anyone else blessed like those two guys were with their blazing, uncommon, fantastic speed?

All the while, my grades dipped, and then continued to dip further, not that I gave a bullfrog's crap. I was sitting tight, waiting. When you're just a little kid, a jigger or whelp like I was, what real importance should one's grades hold, despite what the prim and boring teachers say? And the answer: None. It is more important to dig in the dirt, to tell racy stories, to blow up plaster monsters, to swim in the ocean, and afterward to feel the salt dry on your peeling and tanned back while you're staring at the girls. Also, it is important to always know where your rabbit's foot is before you go to sleep. All of that in itself and taken together is a ton of stuff for any small fry to remember and not forget, or else some unexpected bad thing might happen.

One day, that fall of 1963, to the extreme rear of our crowded classroom, I had positioned myself, the better to steal a sidelong, but lengthy, glance at my new and presumed Sheba, my solidly built paramour or bobbysoxer, Deborah Parker, and her snow-cone shaped boobies. And that day I noticed how they always seemed to be getting better, bigger, and more spectacular with every passing day, so much so that I tasked myself this question: Was it just for me, this delightful and endearing sight, what my dad used to call, with any man's gleeful wink,

"A free view?"

That day toward the end of baseball season, I had asked my teacher, Mrs. Bainbridge, who always wore heavy and thick wool plaid skirts even though it was hot outside, and her bottom was already big enough without her wearing plaid, if I might move closer to the blackboard, the better to see it. Yes, I would miss my Deborah, peering at her, them, but I figured I'd just have to find other, new opportunities, chances for me to be able to leer at her, which from now on would probably only be at recess.

Now, that question of mine serves to any alert teacher as an admonition or red flag or what the heck warning that the student in question must get his eyes checked and soon, pronto. Shake it up! So, it was quickly scheduled, my first eye exam, downtown, across from the La Mar Theater where every Saturday summer day we used to watch Viking movies, endless, brightly colored ones with bloody swords and fancy leather sandals, including those featuring the lovely and underappreciated Rosanna Podesta. She, too, was born in Tunisia, in Tripoli, of our Marine fame.

This was back in the good old days when downtown, you could still buy loose nails at the hardware store, when the barber, an old man named Oscar, never forgot your name, when bread and candy were still made right there in the store, right in front of you, and when the butcher counter still had real sawdust on the floor to soak up the blood and the fat and all the other gut messy drippings. And the butcher, a hairy man named Mr. Bellucci (who had survived all the partigiani chaos in Italy, in the Apennines, exactly 20 years earlier), took his pleasant time to ask my mom how the roast was, and he wasn't talking about her bottom or rump.

Today, just so the story is told full and properly, the same town is full of sunglass and bikini shops, not that I have anything against either, especially the latter, but, for Pete's sake, you can no longer get a fresh, made-right-there hero or hoagie or dogwood, not to save your life.

If you do find a sandwich there today, it is some days old, limp thing with way too much mayonnaise, and some junky piece of meat probably made weeks ago in Lynwood. But, yet again, I digress, since I was about to get my lousy, failing, completely on-the-fritz eyes checked.

So, not long afterward, I get in the eye doctor's chair, and the doc, some smelly dweeb with lots of nose hair, stinky breath, and a plastic sleeve in his chest pocket holding nine pens in case one runs dry—the doc, he has me look through this big black pair of goggles, binoculars, really. And he was asking me, real fast, which sight or view is better, which is worse, back and forth like that, and it was all so fast that soon I got really confused. So, eventually, I must have said the wrong thing and given him the wrong answer. In truth, then, that day I could not see anything well. Everything was blurry! Everything! Right away, the doc is pissed! Suddenly, unexpectedly, he is pissed off at me and mad. He thinks that I'm fooling around, playing him for a stooge or a mickey! So, he calls my mom into the room, and he says to her, real serious like,

"I'm having some trouble with your boy here, Mrs. Martin. He claims he cannot see anything clearly, and that cannot be true, else he would not have been able to find this office or that chair upon which he currently rests."

So, right away, my mom says to me,

"Young man, you do want to hit the baseball, don't you?"

And sure enough, that got my attention, but they were both full of horsepucky. I couldn't see, that is, I could not see clearly.

But, eventually, trying hard and not being quite so nervous, I could make out (using the other meaning) a few things that doc had asked about. Once he looked at me real serious, with my mom standing right there next to us to make sure that I never said, "anything disrespectful or untoward," as Mom would phrase it, and then he asked me,

"Are you telling me the truth there, young fellow, the whole truth?"

And I responded,

"Of course, doctor. The God's own. Always."

I could tell as soon as I said it that he was wondering where the heck I got that phrase from. But, let him wonder. Rats to him, I thought: Rats!

By that time, I was done with the exam, finally. The doc and my mom slunk off into a quiet corner of his office and whispered together there, back and forth in low tones. For myself, I was busy cramming as much of his office candy into my deep pockets as they would allow, carrying it all, and all the while trying to avert the frowning gaze of the office secretary. *She was pretty, even while frowning*, I thought. But back then, I thought all the girls were pretty. As my older brother sometimes used to say to me, acting as a kind of older and advising coach, one scouting for possible female pulchritude, saying,

"She is in the pool," that is, she is included in the pool or serene subset of feminine beauty, the gathering together of all delectable, yet unattainable, women. And the crux of it, my brother advised, was that all women were in the pool. All of them. Every darn one. Why not? Let them all in, and then we can say, rejoicing,

"Let us all go swimming together."

On the way home, I could see that my mom's eyes were moist and teary. She dabbed at their wet edges. Trying to act tough though I was only 12 and weighed only 78 pounds, I told to her to knock off the crying, saying to her,

"When the hell was I ever hurt?"

And then I said to Mom,

"Jax. And God is gracious, and I have never been lonesome in my life."

I don't know why I sometimes call her Jax. It was an odd name for Mom. It must have been one of those chance nicknames that stick like 'Little Colonel' for the Dodger's shortstop, Pee Wee Reese.

Lord knows, kids do unexpected, stupid, and poppycock things sometimes, and so do adults, for that matter, and that is why or how they sometimes call them dolts.

Anyway, as we walked the nine blocks home, she told me that I had some very serious problems with my eyes (desperate, I wondered; is the situation desperate, or is it serious?) and that I needed to carry out vigorous exercises upon them, so that with considerable time they might then strengthen a little, which is what they needed to do; and too, she also told me that shortly, near to a month away, around Thanksgiving of that year, 1963, the year in which my hallowed Dodgers had just won the World Series in 4 straight games with the Yankees only scoring four total runs (the second lowest total ever); and too, not that anyone gives a toot anymore, but in that same year, Tommie Davis, Brooklyn-born yet never playing there, only in LA, won the batting crown for the second year in a row, and in October of the same year old TD, speedy, had set the club's record for RBIs with 153; and I'm thinking of all of this and more as Mom and I walk and talk down the road, that TD's feat and feet were both unbelievable and that he never got the kind of rabid fans' attention that he deserved, no way; and that is when she said, not that I was paying her very close attention, my mom, that is, she telling me that I would soon be getting some thick black glasses, what everybody at school would probably call 'coke bottles' because of how thick they would be sitting there on my little nose; and all of this would be done, carried out, so that I might see, so that I might see better, the better both to hit the baseball and to get the grades.

However, screw them! Screw them with a vengeance squirts! I told my mom I didn't care how thick they were, if I could hit a baseball hard and long and solid and deep to left center (like my man Demeter had done three times that night in April way back in '59) where it would be at least an easy triple for me, no matter how strong the outfielder's arm was.

Dazzling, dangerous 'Big D' had hit them out, three times, all homers, but I'd be just as happy freewheeling it around to third since triples are quite fine and rare, most rare.

Not long afterward on that fourth Friday of November, after my mom got a call from the pretty secretary that my glasses were ready to be fitted (Fitted? Fitted? Did I have to take off all my clothes? Not in front of her! No way in heaven!), I went back to the eye doctor's office.

But, before I went there, I must admit, if truth be told all the way and not just skated around or half muttered, that I first entered Vuckovic's candy shop next door, since I had a few extra clicks of the clock to use up, or time. He was a friend, 'Gary V', we called him, and a good classmate. He was one of those guys always with a smile, and he never took advantage of anyone, never, nor came close to it. However, today, he was in school. Ha! I was 'skipping' or AWOL, because of my eye appointment, and I knew he wouldn't be in the store, like usual, helping his sisters. It was all a family deal, the Vuckovic's candy store, started a few years before I was born. And ahh! Such smells! All the women who worked there were always jolly, like Gary V. was, and a little chubby, what my dad used to call,

"Beaucoup or cats in a sack."

But, grunts and growlers, what the heck! The ladies at the counter usually asked me what it was that I wanted, and so that day I told them,

"A pound of shiny, black jellybeans for my popski, and as much of that delicious mint taffy as this messy wadge of coin, kroner, and pelf will allow."

"Yes, sir, young man. Coming right up! Tout de suite!"

The nice ladies with the big smiles always threw in something extra or magic or special. They said that it was for Tom Jefferson. So, I asked them,

"Tom who?"

And I left the candy store, as usual, with them giggling as I closed the door.

Finally, that Friday around noon, I entered the doctor's office. This time I was glad to see that he was not so grumpy, so quick to anger. He put my new, thick, black glasses on my face, like he was anointing a king, and immediately, because of my puny nose, they slid down, right away, almost to the tip of my small nose. But, after some pushing and pulling and bending, they fit better and no longer slipped down my little nose. He offered me a mirror to look at myself wearing glasses for the very first time, with him saying,

"Well, son. What do you think of yourself with glasses?"

And, right away, I responded,

"I look like a geek, a dweeb, and a twerp has-been all rolled into one, someone low on voltage and ugly to boot. But it doesn't matter, not one whit or measure, doc, because now, with your expert help, I'll be able to hit the ball, maybe not like Davis or Demeter, but well enough, sir, doctor, but well enough."

Yet, little did I know, just then, at that scant and fleeting runaway second, now so many years and miles ago, as I, just a twelve-year-old, was getting out of the tall black leather eye doctor's chair and about to enter the small anteroom where the pretty secretary worked, that I was about to grow older, unalterably, and very quickly so.

I saw her seated there at her desk crying, crying heavily. Tears were gushing out of her green eyes, a deep green the color of the not yet besmirched virginal fields of western Ireland, and the water was gushing out of her eyes fast and hard like someone had just turned on the kitchen tap. Her tears fell heavy and glistening; and they were free-flowing, and dozens and dozens of them, dropping onto her linen blouse, a pretty Derwent green, it recalling innocence and summers spent well before all of this happened, the tears making it, her pretty blouse, all suddenly wrinkled and matted and sodden. Now, I thought speedily then as a guy who never wanted to miss a thing, a young fellow who was always alert or on point, I could see her bra underneath: There it is! Yes! Eureka! I have found it!

She had the clock radio on loudly, and, suddenly almost as an affront or attack, she turned to me, with her eyes all bloodshot and pink and puffy, and announced to me, a stranger,

"President Kennedy has just been shot in Dallas, Texas. He is feared dead. It is most unexpected and sudden. The President is feared dead. No."

She has said that awful word, 'dead', twice close together. And, lastly, that strong word: No. And with that, she wailed deeply and immediately plunged her face forward onto her bare arms flat on her desk and wailed again, this time even more deeply, with her breath catching and her chest heaving. Quickly, surprising me to no end, she raised herself up and asked me patiently,

"What do we believe in now, son? What values do we hold dear? What values do we practice as a nation?"

Before I had a chance to say anything, to try to console her, she returned her wet face to her arms and cried some more, moaning deeply like she was having a bad dream from which he could not awake and shaking her head manically from side to side.

What she had said to me had straightened me up into a soldier's stance, and I was never the same stupid kid again, at least not quite as stupid. For example, from that time forward, I never again made mean comments about Mrs. Bainbridge's wide figure or tried to make her cry, as I had done more than once in the past; but, instead, I thought how she was an excellent, alert Math teacher and that it was she who had first discovered and then informed my parents about my lousy eyes. Therefore, in a real way it was she who had helped me to see better.

As I walked home that day, I saw for my first-time grown men openly and without any shame crying upon the street, 50-year-old men, and women also, all bawling their eyes out, dabbing at them with wet handkerchiefs, even though they would not stop producing tears, uselessly clutching at their damp hankies. One of the men, another stranger, put his hand upon my shoulder and said to me, his eyes ablaze with emotion,

"We need to pray for this country, son. And we must start to do so now. Oremus."

And through all of this, I thought all the Kennedy family members who were left behind, that is, those who survived and were not yet killed or shot. How could they bear this impossible burden? In the face of such an unnecessary tragedy, how could they manage to go on, to continue, to endure? How could they not hate all the citizens of this country when one of them, a moron, a creep, a supreme screwball, for whatever cockeyed, messed up reason, had so brazenly gunned down a good, decent, and smart man who was only attempting to lead us onward, to whatever bright new place that he might find for us. While he was still alive, before we had killed him, I thought then, still surrounded by all the then weeping members of our town (Yes, the emotion by this time had caught up with me also, and I was crying heavy too), that often he had shown with jokes and a cock of his head with what my dad called,

"His shining Irish wit."

And, I thought, President Kennedy never used the words 'serious' and 'desperate' interchangeably since he knew deep in his heart the blackness that all the Irish from the beginning of time used to know: That the world is a brief and difficult way station beset with failure and grief and precious little joy, that it is a voyage full of problems. And he had demonstrated many times that most rare of all the public virtues: Courage.

That night at home, Dad turned to me and said, giving me a small order, "Please, son, don't slouch. Stand up straight, son."

But I could see something deep and sad in his eyes. And that night at the dinner table everyone, my mom and dad, my brother and sister, everybody was quiet. Throughout the whole dinner, my mom silently wept. And my dad, after he had had a couple of glasses of red wine, Zinfandel, his favorite, he said to all of us,

"Now that the foul deed is done, I just hope they get the stupid jerk. However, what I need to know is this: What kind of nation are we now, that we show such a lack of tolerance? To kill someone? Does disagreeing with somebody give a person the right to blast him from behind? He's a coward, a chicken, an imbecilic pansy ass. I bet he's just another idiot cracker from the Deep South, one of those gremlin hairballs that is always happy to marry his little sister. However, will you answer me this: What have we become? What? Where will this violence lead? What September song is this? Tell me! Tell me now, blast it! Tell it to me!"

* * *

Some time passed. It must have been a couple of years. My man, Demeter, named after the male form of the goddess of corn and all fruits, had been traded away from the Dodgers to the Phillies. We were already deep into the '65 season, me and my Dodgers, and Koufax's arm was starting to give him some real trouble. It was on the fritz, on a downhill funeral slide. Whenever he pitched, he put so much torque on it, the way he arched his chest forward even though the ball was still back toward 2nd base, and that dodo bird, Manager Walter Alston, was pitching him in way too many games. There were free-flowing rumors that Koufax could not lift his elbow above his head, just to comb his black hair. I swear that these dodo-bird, jerk ball guys in charge do not understand that it is very easy to over-pitch pitchers, even the great ones; no, scratch that, especially the great ones since they throw harder. I said to myself, since I was thinking out loud: You got that, Sport, or am I going too fast for you?

Soon, that summer the Watts riots came, arrived on the scenes with murders and looting and destruction. Were they expected or not? The god, Zeus, might say but today he cannot be reached. And all the attendant fires and theft and general mayhem just erupted, as if by chance or bad magic.

All of this was happening not very far away from our house. It was very hot that summer and the sprawled city, still languid and reclined, spotted, maculated by wild and smoldering fires across so many of her nooks and crannies, down the narrowest lanes and busiest boulevards, due to the dozens of spontaneous conflagrations she seemed to grow even hotter. The riot there went on for days, a marathon testament to simple, unadorned stupidity, and from our front porch, with little wind from the Pacific, I could see the blanket of smoke resting upon the supine city, like a thick blanket placed upon a tired and resting soldier, one fully exhausted and naturally disinclined to move. It refused to move, and some in the richer suburbs to the north complained about its addition to the merciless, penetrating smog. Yet, through it all, during it, the city, or rather its inhabitants, was most restless and did not sleep. Some refused to sleep at night in fear for their lives.

Others refused to sleep since they wanted the camouflage or guise of night's darkness to begin to loot, rob, and sack their own city, to steal from their own neighbors, cloaking their thieving in the fake, old words of all past robbers and thieves, saying,

"I had to."

Shortly afterward during that most fratricidal summer, wherein brother harmed brother irredeemably and since he would not be caught and brought up on charges, one Saturday afternoon, I was over at Donnie MacPherson's house. We were building models together, I, a ship, the gleaming white Olympia (My 12" version was a small toy compared to the 344 foot long real liner), and he, a monster, The Mummy from the Black Lagoon, who stood almost one foot tall. We were both working hard, concentrating and being quiet, so we could easily hear his father speak from the kitchen,

"These blacks! What are they thinking? And what the hell are they fighting about? That neighborhood once was fine. It was settled first by the Germans and then by the Irish. They kept up their lawns, for Jerry's sake. And, occasionally, they'd apply a coat of paint! Some of those earlier residents engaged in some normal upkeep from time to time. Did you know that Duke Snider, the fantastic and just retired center fielder for the Dodgers, went to Compton High School just a little south of where the riots were? Did you? Huh?"

His wife answered him, saying,

"No, dear. I didn't know that! Would you please calm down a tad? The boys can hear you and they will become upset."

She always smelled so good, Mrs. MacPherson did. Often, she'd make us the best molasses cookies. I can still remember looking at her brown and muscled arms when, wearing one of the sleeveless gingham dresses which were popular at the time, especially in the summertime when she would lean down low, carrying the hot platter of molasses cookies out of the oven. They'd be hot as houses right then out of the oven, like that, and we'd down gallons of cold milk to keep our mouths from getting scorched, burned, or singed.

However, Mr. MacPherson continued,

"I don't give a blast or blinger if they can hear me. Those boys ought to know that the black family is breaking down, and fast. Those folks don't stay married anymore, though they used to. What has changed? Do black women all suddenly smell bad? Drag a leg? Possess bad teeth? But I hear it's mostly the men's fault. What do you say, honey?"

"I say you need to set the table, jiggins."

Later that night, at home, I asked Dad about what Mr. MacPherson had said that day: Was it true? All true?

Dad laughed a little. He said to me,

"That young man reminds me of Churchill's line: 'That man is the only bull I know who carries his own China shop around with him.' I don't truly know, son. Perhaps we ought not to judge others quite so harshly. Are we fit to judge? Are we?"

I said,

"I think not, sir. But, what about the riots, all the protests and the looting and the fires and the moaning and groaning. Is it legit?"

He looked at me evenly and behind his eyes, I could sense his brain working, turning. My dad said nothing for quite some time, looking off into space, and then he said,

"In life, forced with problems, difficulties, adversities, it is easy to complain. Easy. But, what good does it do, son? John Wooden, you know him, the basketball coach at UCLA, tells his players: Don't moan! Don't complain! Rather, use any difficulty to advance, to reach higher. Don't let it knock you down; but get up! The British RAF pilots have a Roman proverb: Ad astra per aspera. To the stars through difficulty. I believe it is also the state motto for Kansas, the state that is the home of Ike and the Jayhawks. Look at it this way, bud: Problems are a gift and therefore our salvation. Make do, son, make do. You have been given more than they, most; so, you must accomplish more. Accomplish! God it? Do you follow me?"

Then I thought to myself, after dad had challenged me for the thousandth time: *Now, where the heck is dinner?* Go to help her who provided you with your birth. That person would be your mother. And give her your full, complete, and docile cooperation. In the kitchen, I say that your mother is sometimes too slow! Too slow! For some daft reason, with my stomach churning and rumbling out of hunger, just then I remembered those hairy forearmed Italian butchers who used to tease mom by saying to her,

"Did someone say: Roast? Rump? Tender? Moist?"

My father, I now think, that day long ago in the summer of 1965, would have been 51 years old pretty much on the button. In other words, he would have been at the same age as most generals are when they report to war. If a general cannot do something well by then, by that time, the chances are he never will, and he then would be washed up, nullified, or maybe given an easy desk job back home. My dad, once he had looked up at me during his 'Don't moan. Don't complain' talk and in that quick instant he had appeared to me to be old. And then, within an instant, he smiled at me, particularly at his central word of advice to his son: 'Accomplish' and all the years of age and their price or toll cast or enforced him instantly had evaporated, gone away, and his brown eyes sparkled richly with the uncontested glee of suddenly recaptured youth. At that time, he would have agreed with any shirttail cousin, and also with any general just before out in the field near to a river, next to trees, and who then says to his aide-de-camp or lieutenant that,

"I'm a lucky son of a bitch and I should never be sad about anything ever again."

As it does inexorably with neither trepidation nor pause, more time passed. My Dodgers ended up winning gloriously the World Series that late fall of 1965, beating the Orioles of Baltimore. After that, it looked to me and to many fans that the Dodgers were set or primed or ready to commence a glorious dynasty of victory; that is, that soon enough the sages, and peers, those in the know in the baseball world would soon begin to compare the team with that other pre-eminent baseball outfit out of New York, saying: Yes, they have the speed with Wills and the Davis brothers, power with the Gargantuan Frank Howard, and an overpowering quartet of pitchers with your young man Sandy Koufax, Don Drysdale, Claude Osteen, and the just-turned-30 Johnny Padres, the hero of Brooklyn's only World Series victory in 1955.

Yet, even with all that good, if not impeccable logic, such a dynasty of overwhelming success was not to be! Why not? It turned out that Sandy would retire right after the '66 season, saying that his long, left arm was shot, done, shutdown, and that many days it hurt so badly, so acutely, that he had to rely upon endless cortisone shots just to function.

Also unexpectedly, soon, that is, not much more than two weeks into the 66 season, after only 17 days, on May 1, 1966 (It, May Day, usually is a day of innocence and promise, but not that day, not that day), Tommie Davis, the team's best hitter, sliding hard into 2nd trying to break up a double play, he broke both his leg and his ankle. In an instant, his blazing speed was gone for good, and a sure Hall of Famer's career suddenly truncated, curtailed. Such a bad and unfortunate incident can take place in the blink of any eye, in an electrical flash, in less time than it takes to make the Sign of the Cross. The young fellow from Brooklyn simply was never the same, never. Only 27 years old at the time of the accident, Davis had lost that small step, that subtle extra edge, that infinitesimal thing that all athletes need or crave and must possess if they want the chance to be the very best. Eventually, the Dodgers lost all possible faith in him and traded him away, and he ended up playing for an astounding 10 major league teams, still the world record for the most traveled ballplayer.

Soon, too, about that same time, especially when one looks back carefully upon this transformation, society began to change, to morph towards the indefensible, to engender and feed aberrant and controlling vices. Incrementally, for example, divorces became no longer rare. Why? If a fellow is tired of the babe, he goes down the road. I asked that simple question then and I ask the same question now.

This was a question that I, then a precocious new teenager, needed to ask because the birth control pill had just been invented a few years earlier. The pill was available pretty much to all the eager beavers like me who no longer had to fear getting caught in a compromised position, i.e., with one's pants down.

About that time, as well, certain relatively untested recreational drugs (Who in Sam Hell came up with that lame moniker?) appeared, and surprisingly to some, they were swiftly praised as safe and life-enhancing. Right away and fundamentally scarred of them, I asked, myself, saying aloud,

"How do they know these things? How do we know that such-and such is true?"

And, thirdly, about that same time, finally and perhaps most terribly (That ominous word, terrible, derives from the Latin word, terrere: To frighten), our country, impossibly and improbably misled, installed a rusty bear-trap upon her own ankle, a musty and mean bear-trap from which one might flee with considerable difficulty, a bear-trap called Vietnam. The country would become a place of quicksand and malaise and corruption. And the long war in that country would not be our salvation, but instead would lead to four dismal results: Dead bodies, long-lasting drug problems, the first cases of homelessness, and the enervation of the individual and national will.

I can remember another general, Westmoreland, not an old type who fought in combat, but today's younger version of the same, so he is an officer who fights mostly with public relations, graphs, projections, sound bites, practiced gestures, and phony demeanor, which is something always feigned and full of guile. In those early days of the war, the newest, yet not the finest version of a soldier, kept saying to President Johnson,

"We need 50,000 more troops to achieve success. I swear to you, sir. A maximum of 75,000. And that will be it, sir, the final extent of our future deployments, that much I will swear to you, sir."

But, next month, set your watch, smoke stacker, he would be asking the commander-in-chief for more soldiers. And Johnson, increasingly grudgingly, would grant the general his request, give in to the fruitless escalations leading nowhere, and accede. Did President Johnson ever deeply question General Westmoreland, asking him how he knew for certain that something in the future might indeed happen? Without these probing and deliberate questions, and although, of course, we did not grasp it at the time, we were slipping toward complete disaster, falling into a profound fissure of ambiguities and endless doubts, falsely committing ourselves by our mounting arrogance to this mocking or ersatz war, one that we were not prepared to fight, for a people who did not want us there and who, even today, we could not even begin to know or understand.

All of this was unknown to us at the time since we did not possess the skill to ask the right questions and then listen to the answers.

My father, forever the proud Fenian fighter, always enjoyed a bit of joisting during our conversations. By this time, I rightly knew that I was lucky to have a father who truly enjoyed a lively repartee with his son. The two of us had begun the practice of nightly debates at the dinner table. We would tackle a wide range of questions from,

"Who is the best boxer, pound for pound?" to, "Why shouldn't welfare have a built-in terminus for single, unmarried men?" and everything in between. For some reason one night, feeling his oats more than a little, Dad asked me this pointed question,

"Why don't we just go kick some ass, some tail, wallop them? Son, why don't we fight this darn war like we want to win it instead of pussyfooting around?"

Yet, in a flash, as if in the flash of war, like the explosion of a mortar shell on the edge of the forest, his vision would soar well beyond that simplest of dreams, and he would admit, announcing the bare, unadorned truth in the next breath,

"Hell: the Vietnamese. They don't want us there. No way. Whom can we trust? General Nguyen Cao Ky? Nguyen Van Thieu? Who among them is telling us the full and unvarnished truth? Who among their leaders doesn't lie, hedge, prevaricate? Did you know that seven levels of honesty exist? Which level of honesty are we working on over there, which one is operating? Which?"

But what could I, a tad or cadet of 15, clueless, gormless and irresolute, say to him? He looked to me, little me, for help, assistance, and that would have been in the wrong direction. That day he was about as exasperated, apoplectic, pissed off with raving, ranting, simple anger as I had ever seen him. Why? The answer is an easy one to find: The idea of his county losing any war was antithetical to everything in his stern and rugged Midwestern character.

However, whenever he thought about Westmoreland and his constantly evolving notions of the truth, Dad instantly mentioned the other 'W' man: Coach Wooden, the humble coach from a small town in Indiana who stipulated to his players all the time this simplest of rules,

"Don't lie. Tell the truth."

My dad would incorporate the coach's maxims, his sayings, and his 15 steps for success into his rants, speeches, one-way dialogues, and then add, in an almost manic leer,

"Are we not going to sleep in this country, son? Are we? Tell the truth! Too much rack time, boss? Dunkirk is here, now! We are dumb and every day getting dumber. Dumb!"

During some of his rails, rants, I was convinced he was on the close verge of blowing his cork, ending it all by anger's blowzy accident, and that he'd soon topple over like a felled tree and be near dead from a massive coronary, before he hit the ground.

Yes, we had discussed the change in warfare and the massive shift in tactics and strategy. But, beyond that, he wondered out loud whether we still possessed the simple will to win, and to dad that lone factor was always the most important one. He instructed me many times that that is what it takes to win a war. He worried about our focus, our concentration. He would bellow to me,

"As we go into this battle, this necessary solitude, which is war, we must not go astray. Never! Why are we there?

"Earlier, both President Eisenhower and France's General De Gaulle had told us not to get involved in an Asian jungle war, but did we listen to them? Did we? All the proper warnings signs simply handed to us were manifestly ignored. That French Colonel Charles Piroth fought well in Vietnam back in the 50s, but still got the loss in battle handed to him. Do we know our own history anymore?

"And you can forget about Raoul Salan, the sleazy French general. Recall that clever Vietnamese fellow, the self-taught General Vo Nguyen Giap: He took the high ground since the dumb bunny French were too slow to seize it. Patton said to never let the enemy pick the high ground, never.

"That reminds me of the Battle of Gettysburg and Major John Buford smartly seizing the high ground the night before the contest commenced. Do we think that we are so much smarter than these people? Do we think, therefore, that it would be impossible for us to lose? Is it not a growing arrogance which compels us to this war's conclusion? Is it?"

My old man was really getting steamed. I realized that Dad knew the history of Vietnam better than some of our generals, military advisors who took way too many things for granted. Once more time, I was afraid he was going to hit the deck with a myocardial infarction or some enormous stroke, which would leave my dad forever enfeebled. Then, suddenly and not to mutter, he turned toward me and nearly screeched, pleading,

"Yes. Yes. You probably think, buddy, that I do not understand that war has evolved. I know all that, whelp, since we already went over that. So, here is the deal, one simply put: The USA doesn't lose wars. We must be prepared to fight and fight fully. These Vietnamese on both sides are playing us for the mickey, the fool, and, since we have acted as fools, we have obliged them. Perhaps, as Ike foretold in his final speech as president, the military industrial complex runs the show. Why, our own Central Intelligence Agency helped to arrange the assassination of Ngo Dinh Diem, the first president of South Vietnam on November 2, 1963, and then walked away it, such an evil act, washing their hands like Pontius Pilate might have done, as if they had just finished eating a bowl of ox tail soup.

"Tanglefoot, the good old USA more and more is looking like some sort of weak sister, an empty suit, or pansy. We must be ready to get the job done!"

For someone like dad who had survived the Great Flu Epidemic, the Great Depression, and the Great World War II, the treacherous circumstance into which by our own actions we had propelled ourselves made him disconsolate, immeasurably disconsolate. It was a good thing that it was a Friday. Dad sank deeper and deeper into the red leather chair that was his (and his father's) favorite before him, and then he took greedily and deep, since it was Friday and he needed it, a long draught of scotch, like my contesting Caledonian grandpa might have done, and then, after starring off in space toward the heavens for some time he toddled like the old sailor he was off to sleep. After his long speech, he had deserved and earned this small rest.

* * *

So, our cities continued to decline into rank savagery, morasses of drugs, places of weakness, enervation, and sin. Government did little or nothing, or by putting in place stupid public policies whose results were fully unforeseen, it actively encouraged what became known as 'The White Flight'. As a nation we gave ourselves wholly over to the rampaging notion of real estate speculation: People could make so much money by doing so very little! Metropolises, cities, towns forming communities, and the smallest spot not even qualifying to be called a burgh—all gave themselves over to the mostly white realtors' irresistible itch to subdivide land, to promote migratory flight from the urban to the suburban, or from the farm to the motor home whereby the dairyman, for example, who had worked all his hard life there and whose children do not want that fatiguing life, might cash in.

Many did indeed cash in. White Flight (not a Patti Page song) suggests that as soon as a section of a city declines, it will be left for those darker skinned, and there, they will find their own way. The white man will leapfrog over the shuttered and dilapidated factories, failing tenements, and bankrupt shops in favor of the suburban, thereby creating the ghetto and, at the same time, and swiftly, leaving it behind. Accordingly, he will not have to witness all the known depravities, such as prostitution, drug havens, and the endless acts of random violence. Indeed, more than likely, once he has left the city, he will no longer even think of the urban centers since the freeway will have bypassed them. Those who caused the blight will no longer see it. Most of our cities were better off when I was born than they are today, a deplorable state or condition caused by people only. People did all of this.

Part of this harmful exodus was fueled by 14-cents-a-gallon gasoline and the foolish notion that that low price would stay in place forever.

Part of this harmful exodus was fueled by a growing government's near-infinite need for always more cash, its operators connived and conniving, thinking that if a small zoning change were needed to bring it more cash, so that government might be bigger, always bigger, so be it.

Part of this harmful exodus was fueled where we lived by glad-handing, in everyone's pocket Mayor Sam Yorty of Los Angeles who never said,

"No," to a business deal, no matter how corrupt, if the city on the opaque face of things made money. He did not think much about the quality of growth, only its quantity, and with his near-unlimited power, he made many friends green and happy.

Here I might insert that I understood the essential corruption of that town before I had pimples. I recognized that this sort of rampart real estate speculation was temporarily good for a few, but that it was untenable, like building a tall brick wall with overly sandy mortar, and that it would, therefore, fall; but, this before that, when the symptoms were not readily apparent, an undetected weakness would set in and, once it started to collapse, the disintegration of the wall could not be stopped.

I think of all this now since I recall one night many years ago. It was another Friday night, and the Vietnam War was starting to completely and irretrievably bust apart our country, to cleave it into two parts, sectors that have not been united since that time. Dad, as usual, was getting pretty worked up, or steamed, saying in a loud voice,

"Florence. Florence! We left the city! After your friend, Yorty, makes all his dirty deals. His real name is this: 'You scratch my back and I'll scratch yours.' Continually, due to his grifting machinations, his sleazy backroom deals, we leave, depart, get out of Dodge, and leave behind a colossal mess. Why do we let these places deteriorate, run downhill, go down the crapper? Why? That is how Watts happened. Damn!"

My mom, once again, tried to placate or mollify his mood, to assent to it, all the while shielding her tender offspring from his more vitriolic outbursts. She said,

"Edward, dear, please. Watch your language. The children."

"Oh, cram it, Florence. These little and innocent dingleberries need to grow up a little. Sooner or later, they will be there, to see it all, the horrendous difficulties, too many difficulties, and, Holy Moses, we must prepare them well. We must do so! It is our job to do so. I want them to grasp now how the self-promoting real estate interests have been running the show here nearly forever. The cities in this once-golden state sprawl all over the place, and farmers are forced out of business so some lazy ass gritter can made a big profit; and every day this happens, every day. Do you want to get your tomatoes from Mexico, sprout? But, do you know that the farmers there put human excrement on them as fertilizer?"

Right away, I howled at this one. I knew what the word meant but I'd never heard it out loud. Excrement! Excrement! What a fancy word! I tingled and shook with glee, mirth. Yet, Dad would not stop, and charged ahead, saying,

"Have you, rubes, ever seen the movie, The Treasure of the Sierra Madre? It's what we've done. It's all about greed, plain-old, muscle in, on-the-sly greed. I'm talking about the kind of coarse impulse which has made Los Angeles, the city of the angels where all you fellows were hatched, the unplanned, ugly, and sprawling mess that it is today. All based on fifteen-cent gasoline. Bogus! An improper model! Improper! And then you've got your so-called farmers, the fake ones, those who buy land cheap, and then insidiously 'play poor' so that they can cash in for the big payola. Gyp bastards. Stinking cheats who'd be happy to sell their own grandma for 10 bucks. Hell, no. What am I saying? Five! Five! Why, look at all the grand baseball ballparks of yesteryear that have gone away for this same lousy reason: Speculation! Money! It rules the land, rules it, I say. Shibe, Nicolette, the Polo Grounds, Griffith, Ebbetts, Sportsman's Park in St. Louis which was demolished just this year, and I'm sure that I'm forgetting a dozen. A dozen! And all for the same lousy reason: Easy money. We've replaced them with all these ugly cookie-cutter jobs."

My mom, by then, clearly had to slow him down,

"Edward, please eat your supper. The beans will be cold."

And, right away, in less time than it takes for a high, rising Don Drysdale fastball to reach the plate, Dad says to Mom and all of us kids,

"Well, I'm not doing so. I'm hot, Florence. Hot! Damn hot!"

However, he did cool for a few moments, eating some beans spiced with ham, slurping back and down some delicious and tannic Barbera, the wine reminding him of ripe damson plums, as he was pausing to swallow, to think, and to organize his wide-ranging mind. You could see his brain working, sorting itself out, ticking away like the best Swiss clock. And then he said,

"You know that Kennedy fellow, Bobbie, that friend of yours and the one whom they call the ruthless one? I think that he may have something good with these Enterprise Zones that he keeps talking about. He says to all of us: 'Fix a place. Don't desert it.' Simple enough. He's been to the worst of the cities: Detroit, Philly, and maybe the worst of them all, Bedford-Stuyvesant in

Brooklyn. He may have something. But he'll have to put in charge scores of ramrods, do you hear me, scores of Patton, Truscott, and Harmon ramrods if he ever wants to get anything done. But here's the question, my little biters, gathered around my ankles: Do they, those needed and unwavering ramrods, exist anymore? Do they?"

And only then, finally, Dad quieted himself and he did not speak again for the rest of the evening.

* * *

All through those years of my now long-distant youth, I could not get the death of our president, John Kennedy, out of my head. Even then, I wondered: How could it have happened? Blinkingly, trying to see, I tried to see clearly the answer to the question: What sort of nation are we wherein this vile and hateful act might occur?

And in the process of trying to comprehend the awful event, subcutaneously, that is, just under the skin and without me knowing it, I understood only one thing: Someone or some unforeseen, yet predictable, force had determined that it was perfectly acceptable to kill a president, any president, if he did not agree with or carry out the killer's aims. Thus, rank personal desire reigned supreme, and became paramount, a corrosive force outside of all commandments and normal strictures. Thus, a chaotic rabble was unleashed, one full of contempt and tumult and no respect. Selfishness arose, mocking President Kennedy's admonition to all Americans given during his famous Inaugural Address delivered on January 20, 1961,

"Ask not what your country can do for you—Ask what you can do for your country."

Therefore, after his assassination, doubting meanness began to lurk about our culture, questioning suspicions were raised, and coarse assumptions spoken and widely promulgated, all factors pulling Americans apart, separating one from the other. Almost overnight, and not incrementally, we were no longer automatically knitted together. Therefore, strangers at bus stations or ballparks no longer joked with each other. Separations grew: Young from old, white from black, rich from poor. At some indeterminate point in those years, we no longer pushed each other to be smarter, better, more articulate, faster but, instead, we started to tear each other down, to declaim and defame, to stab others in the back since it was both possible and easy to do so, and unsurprisingly in that process, we began to destroy ourselves and our nation. Later, when technology arrived, the separations became wider and the estrangements even more severe. Where once we, as a unified, protective people, had fought vigorously toward common goals which would serve a common benefit: The Flu, the World War II, the Depression, now we fought only for the most private glories or with each other.

Given this new cultural context what happened a few years later was not surprising. Just as the new baseball season was starting (Boston's Fenway probably still had dirty spring snow on the ground), it was no surprise that on April 4, 1968, as he stood on the 2nd floor of the Lorraine Motel in Memphis, Tennessee, Dr. Martin Luther King, Jr. was gunned down by another nut head, another white cracker idiot. Question: Why didn't he just leave Dr. King alone? Answer: He did not want to. We may conclude that the killer, driven by desire and with no functioning conscience, thought that he owned the intrinsic right to kill another man.

Immediately, violent racial riots broke out across the country, especially those cities with large black ghetto populations like Detroit and Newark. For a time, it seemed that the whole nation was on the verge of a huge and merciless conflagration, one that it then would not be able to extinguish.

That night, campaigning for the Democrat nomination for the Presidency, Robert Kennedy arrived in Indianapolis, Indiana. Knowing that most of the largely black crowd had not yet heard of the eloquent leader's death, while he did, Kennedy felt the heavy and cruel responsibility to so inform them. But, how to do it? How? Before speaking, he must have wondered: What keen words ought to be employed? What precisely can I say to soften or mollify the severe blow that the members of the audience are about to experience?

Presidential candidate Robert Kennedy told them that their charismatic and decent and thoughtful leader had been shot dead by another wingnut. Pointedly, he did not inform them that the suspect was white. All were shocked, stunned, and angry; too, instantly some were frozen in rage, and who could blame them? Yet, that night Robert Kennedy, as if arriving out of heaven's blue, was imbued with magical, or zauberhaft qualities. He was a lyrical, yet common-sense pragmatist who knew instinctively how to help these people and how not to pander to them, which is assuredly what most other speakers also running for office would have done.

So, Kennedy would not create any farther polarization; he would not add greater fuel to the fire, and he would not help to instigate a riot. He would not feed their new and righteous anger since he understood that it could quickly transform itself to a gnawing hate, which is something that only brings unhappiness.

He witnessed their palpable grief yet tried to assuage it. Most speakers, again, would not have done so.

Instead, he appealed for understanding and compassion, love and wisdom: All the old words. He told them to not grow greater grief or feed rising anger. Put aside, he said to them, as least as best you can and with God's grace, a force for good won via constant prayer, your grievances and all thoughts of revenge or retribution. Consider, at least for a time, forgiveness. Finally, by memory he quoted the Greek poet and dramatist, Aeschylus, whom he had carefully studied after his brother's painful death and who many centuries ago advised us all how best to handle a frightening and compounding loss. Only a wise man, one rare and close to heaven, to God's always open ear, could have delivered without notes such a wise and impromptu speech.

Moreover, and here is the key, the linchpin, the nexus, nut or knot: Those gathered there knew instinctively that Robert Kennedy could speak to them, to tell them what to do and how to think because of what earlier had happened to his brother, Jack. He, too, had been senselessly murdered. (Aren't all killings senseless, or nearly so?). After his brother's death, Robert had gone through an intense period of deep depression and remorse and a near-graceless doom, until he asked God for help. This sadness and gloom weighed on his soul for years and never really left him. It explains the frequent look of wistfulness on his face, and how sometimes he would appear profoundly distracted, perhaps thinking again of what might have been if his brother had lived.

Now, the people to whom he spoke would have to embark on the same long trek, a similar path. They would have to figure out how to get over the death of Doctor King. They knew that; and that is why and how they could trust him. That somber Indiana night Robert Kennedy showed again that he possessed the tough mettle and demonstrated the simple determination necessary for any leader.

By this time, Robert Kennedy was no longer just a preening or pleasing politician; rather, with assiduous and carefully applied effort, he had morphed or reinvented himself as a true leader. Bobbie knew, only because of what happened to his brother, that acceding to grievances of all manner or of any sort only gives mean circumstance the upper hand. Then, it tends to rule us, to take over. Hates makes for mounting unhappiness. And in the process, we become small.

By that time, the crucial year of 1968, as I was about to enter my final year in high school, Robert Kennedy strongly opposed the Vietnam War. He had taken that position grudgingly (Did that anti-war strategy contravene his natural aggressiveness?) He thought to himself: *With so many of our cities moribund and dying, increasingly full of drugs, violence, and grinding poverty, can we afford to be the world's bully or policeman?* In time, he resigned as Attorney General of the United States, declared for and won the Senate seat from New York (resisting the carpetbagger label, and living in the same Long Island town, Glen Cove, as had once that old Dodger, 3-time MVP, catcher Roy Campanella), and eventually after President Johnson abdicated on March 31, 1968, Senator Robert Kennedy declared himself as a candidate for the Presidency.

Yet, a pervasive melancholy still marked his campaign. Haunted by such tragedy, he did not often smile broadly. He did not tell many jokes. Often on the dais, his Irish face would become occluded, his visage lost in thoughts of sharpest tragedy, his mind and emotions drifting to some better and less savage place a million miles away.

During the campaign he continually spoke about how, as Americans, we must come together as one people, that we must stop attacking each other. He was talking not only about the race issues, but about all the other, growing fractures: The poor and the rich, the young and the old, the white and the black, and the rural and the urban. He understood that a current of selfishness was beginning to flood into the consciousness of our nation, that notion that each man is only out for himself, and right away, instinctively, he railed against that uncharitable idea.

For example, Bobbie, not afraid to antagonize powerful and wealthy farmers, sided with Cesar Chavez in the grape fields of California: Kennedy backed Chavez in his uphill battle to secure better wages and improved working conditions for all farm workers.

Today, my hunch is this: I think he grasped that Americans, because of that growing selfishness, were starting to lose all our values. My intuition is that he knew that without commandments, God telling us what to do and no matter how many times we fail, that we will all be lost, gone astray, haywire, pursuing various vices on the long and crooked road to perdition. His faith, always present but by necessity having grown steely and much stronger after the death of his brother, John, allowed him to apprehend this apparent conundrum: Absent rules, we will all be ruled only by rank and always changing desires.

Some people today seem to have forgotten that Robert Kennedy was a vigorous Catholic who believed not in the supremacy of the individual, as our culture now dictates, by in the rules of the Church. From that idea it follows that Kennedy would have understood why there were so many sad Americans, Americans who believe in nothing save their own benefit, those who may have lost, temporarily at least, all faith.

Due to his genetics, his natural faith, and because of that process of a deeper faith that his mother had engendered within him as a child and which his brother's death had catalyzed (for it was either that good option or the deepest blue), Kennedy had a moral toughness a mile wide. He knew that all political questions have at their core a lively and central moral component. And he did not try to act as so many do today (regarding abortion, sex trafficking, or the Wall Street scandals, among many other issues) that it, that ethical component, does not exist or impinge.

Turning once again toward the war in Vietnam, public sentiment more and more began to go against it. Senator Eugene McCarthy of Wisconsin (and another Irishman) was perhaps the first and most vociferous public official to speak out against it, stating the obvious: That is their war to fight, and not ours. Yet, still, many in the country did not agree with Kennedy's opposition to it, thinking that once you start something, you must finish it, see it through to the last olive. They felt that to change course in the middle of the war would be like swapping canoes in the middle of the river or a prize fighter taking a fall. In the beginning of the end of the war, my parents also thought that way, at least as I now attempt to recall their views and catalogue them for posterity through the considerable swirling mists of time.

One day during the Oregon primary campaign, my father turned to me and said,

"Your man, Kennedy, the so-called ruthless pit-bull, is still making a hell of a fuss regarding those Enterprise Zones. And if he's not careful, he'll put everyone to sleep on that one. Most people aren't that intellectual. Your friend,

Kennedy, makes a darn good case for them. However, I happen to agree with him on that issue. Yes, I do."

Both Kennedy and my dad understood that we cannot keep closing factories and abandoning our cities to create urban areas blighted by sporadic crime, spreading homelessness, random violence, or the latest drugs. Rather, we must repair the cities, mostly by tax incentives and public/private partnerships. By force of will, if nothing else, we must rebuild them, now. We have had years to do so, and not much has happened that is good. To dally or to allow an urban area to fester unattended will only make things worse which is, of course, pretty much has happened in my lifetime. Look at Detroit, consider Philadelphia, and ponder the collapse of once-beautiful Baltimore.

Few recall today that Kennedy lost the Oregon primary. Had his campaign lost some of its focus? Was his heart and mind not fully engaged? Was he too wistful? Too sad? Perhaps. In any case, at that key point in history, remarkably it was the first time that a Kennedy had lost an election, a fact which must have shaken all those on his staff, including the senator himself, more than a little. A Kennedy lost? Unbelievable! Quickly, though, all the sleepers awakened since the California primary was just around the corner.

* * *

Back then, most of us, pimply, nerdy guys just like me, fifteen years old or close to it, driving a motorcycle but not yet a car or truck, within what is called by sociologists 'my peer group', we were the awkward ones who still worked in the orchards and fields. Yet, just a few years later a proper white boy would no longer do that sort of tiring, menial work, since within an eye's blink (dictated by what unseen god?) that sort of painstaking work would be considered demeaning, déclassé, ignoble, or pain-in-the-rear employment suitable only for those with a darker skin tone.

We worked with oranges and lemons, mostly, but there was one, large grapefruit orchard up on the steep and twisting Foothill Lane where some Jewish people had a summer camp for the city kids. The owners probably thought and said out loud,

"Give them some air! Some clean air! Their young lungs could use an airing out! For those city kids completely unused to exercise, it will be such a nice change from the smog of the city!"

So, my high school buddies, we nerd balls, rubes, and John Farmers, we irrigated the trees, fixed water lines, fertilized with urea, and applied minor elements in that special, precise, and magical time just before bloom, so that the tree would set a full and bounteous crop of fruit. It did not make any sense to just grow too many green leaves and not enough oranges to pay the bills and more. Usually, though, we sprayed weeds since that was a mindless and endless job commensurate with our limited abilities. To kill the weeds, we sprayed straight diesel fuel laced with a surfactant to encourage its uptake. The spray wand always leaked, due to a bad or pinched gasket, and, accordingly, by the end of the day, my jeans would sodden with the grimy spilled diesel, and Mom would have to wash them separately to keep them from contaminating an entire load of laundry.

Even though many of us were underage, say, 14, 15, or 16, when we started these jobs which taught us two key things: How to follow orders and that we were all willy-nilly team players on America's workforce. Nobody bothered about child labor laws. Were they ever in enforced? Screw it! Who cares? Crap! Chowderhead! Listen, Lester: Who gives a darn? Do you think life is a picnic, Myrtle? On the level, most of my bosses did not care one whit or twinkle if they were breaking some stupid labor laws prohibiting full-time employment for fifteen-year-olds since they knew already that such laws were for city people only. Besides, by blazes, certain menial farm tasks simply had to be done, accomplished! Anyway, all my bosses treated me beyond fairly. Soon enough, within a couple of years only, times would change so that it would no longer be common to find a young, college-inclined white youth working in the fields, because he had been entirely supplanted by young men, single men or solteros mostly, from Culiacan, Durango, and Mazatlán. However, that discussion is another long and sad tale quite beyond the reach of this one.

Still, I can recall it closely now: That soft evening in early June, after an early dinner, I had gone back out into our orchard to change an irrigation set. As one of my bosses, Mr. Banks, used to say both to me and the trees,

"There is no sense in irrigating one tree two times, with its neighbor getting stuffed. I want no one out there short-sheeted. Understand? Hear me?"

Obviously, he used to talk to the trees like they were people, his children. But, what the dingus, there are worse foibles. I am thinking that when I get to his ripe age, I'll probably be just as bonkers, crazed, if not worse than that old cracker, wheeze hound himself.

It probably took me less than an hour to change out the irrigation set, and I came out of the orchard with the sun slanting hard behind my back, now that it was just past dusk, to watch a little TV. Since I was a teenager, I did not give a rat's fart or a wisenheimers' whistle that my wet, muddy boots made a complete mess on the floor. I flipped on the set (since there were no remotes back then), and there he was looking good, swell: Robert Francis Kennedy standing behind a microphone in a huge dining room at the Ambassador Hotel on Wilshire Boulevard. Right away, I thought about how in the late 30s and all through the 40s, whenever they had gathered up a little scratch, my mom and dad would drive up there to the Miracle Mile, to go to the Coconut Grove nightclub right there at the hotel, to listen to the big band sounds, and too, to watch and to study the already practiced and preening celebrities of the day who would be, by today's entirely debased standards, considered as kings and queens.

He looked pretty good, but skinny. He had lost weight. His cheeks were sunken. You could tell that he had not had much to eat lately. I wondered if his body mass had not shrunk somewhat under the constant travel and the still-remembered and never-shrinking grief of his brother's death? I noticed too that he wore a simple blue and white tie, and I figured that the blue for him symbolized freedom (all those tall-masted ships sitting in the harbor getting ready to sail within hours upon the open and benevolent seas) and the white forecast purity or his soul's intrinsic integrity.

Overall, though, he looked pretty good, alert, experienced. I thought to myself: *At last, here's the kind of ready-to-go, and no baloney and hokum guy who knows the inning and knows the score.* Therefore, we could confidently entrust this country to him, and he would not screw it up; moreover, he would not succumb to beckoning corruption, and he would not create a rancid hash. Even though enemies of various stripes, all sorts of fearless legions, are right now advancing toward us, I thought, he could well and quickly lead us out of this advancing and expanding trouble. Like all volunteers, all those genetically inclined and groomed for leadership, with a full heart, Robert Kennedy is ready to step forward. He is now able to shoulder any heavy burden. This guy knows, I then thought, how to bring people together. So, he understands the small point of this tale: That a certain kind of special magic happens when people are united, knitted together by special unspoken bonds, rather than separated.

When I examined his wistful face, I thought again about how Kennedy had grappled with his grief for months, years; to conquer it, I knew that he had made a serious study of the philosophies of the Greeks and of Albert Camus; how he had delved into parts of the Bible, especially the Book of Job; and how he had expanded his faith because he had to, because such a job was required. I studied how he had evolved, pragmatically, as any good soldier might have done, as needed, to be better able to fight tomorrow's difficult and unseen and unpredictable battles. Thus, I thought, he is someone who can learn on the job, a very useful trait if one is president.

All of this and more, I mused upon, not really listening to his acceptance speech (Yes, he won; he had won) which was predictable, stock fare. I was watching his eyes, his shrouded eyes. They were still most sad and distant, and his unruly shock of thick brown hair, which covered his eyes a little, preventing us from any further privileged glimpses of his soul. Perhaps, I thought, he does not wish to be truly seen by others. Perhaps he, more than anything else, really wishes to be alone with his pregnant wife and family. And who can blame him? I got the feeling that he was a reluctant leader, someone like our first president, General George Washington, who had to be pushed or forced into office.

But, just then, startling me out of that wandering revelry, I heard him say to the festive gathered crowd,

"Now, it's on to Chicago, and let's win there!"

He gave a short, choppy wave of his hand to the pressing and exuberant crowd and disappeared into the massive throng of people. I recognized Rafer Johnson and Rosie Greer, protectors standing tall among the happy gathering, as two large and very strong black men and athletes.

They must be guarding him to make sure that nothing bad would happen to him, like had happened with his brother, protecting him from some new guy off his rocker, of which we did not seem to have a shortage, some pansy-ass wingnut, another cowardly idiot who might be lurking there in the shadows, just trying to pull a fast one.

Just then, when it was just after midnight, a long series of gunshots rang out, and, since I'd been around guns some, I knew immediately that Senator Robert Kennedy was a goner, packed up, deep-sixed, and toast. With that many shots fired, I understood right away, one of them certainly would be fatal. So, we had killed another good man, the third. As he lay on the floor of the kitchen prep area mortally wounded, his last words were,

"Are any of my people hurt?" since he cared more about others than himself. Once again, that idea of selflessness and its counterpoint come to the fore.

And thus, it started for me, from that June 4, 1968, evening onward, an odyssey of examination, a long period of reflection and soul-searching, one beginning with the simplest question,

"What kind of country are we if we keep killing our best men?"

Immediately, I went across the house to see my folks, and, after I had told them what had taken place, they were both sad, dumbstruck, troubled. My dad seemed dazed, as if from a long lack of sleep or some sort of nervous system melancholia. He said to me,

"Well, we killed another good one, chum."

He left the room for bed. And so, for the last, fifty-odd years, ever since that ugliest of nights, I have been trying to calculate how all these bad things could have happened and how the history of our nation might have been drastically different had we simply let these three good men live.

In that process, let us ask ourselves an obvious question: What has changed, so utterly, in our national character? Once we cared more about overreaching and majestic national goals; however, today, or so it seems, we are driven by wholly private desires and motives. Were we not once unified fighters, determinedly inclined toward victory over a common enemy, or the best course of action for the greatest number of people, what used to be called, now almost anachronously, 'the common good'?

That united direction, to achieve a goal, an exercise rooted in discipline, has this habit of mind not been forever lost? Do we not, instead, wallow in a series of small, private, un-national interests? Where is the old form of leadership? I fear that these current internecine battles, those that splinter rather than unite, may be the end of us.

Robert Kennedy and his brother, John Kennedy, and Dr. King, Jr. believed in unity and civility.

They thought that people could disagree, but that they had to do so respectfully, not disdainfully; and, all the while, that we must remain one people, one nation, knitted together in a common fabric of humanity. I think that all three men, good leaders all, would look at today's fundamental fractiousness, the fact that we can now barely speak to each other, and that they would be aghast, appalled, and repulsed.

If they were alive, what else might they say to us? Those three darkest days: What if history could, by sanctity, some sort of God's magic or enchanting Zauber, be erased, reversed, and scrubbed clean of those three cruel deeds? What if one could turn back the merciless, steadily clicking clock to a greater sanity in which those three equally senseless killings had not taken place? What if those three men had been allowed by God, not man, to fulfill their individual destinies? Yes, I know that some may say that such speculation is futile, but to me, it is not useless to conjecture, imagine and dream, all the time thinking: What might have been.

Since the sixties when all three of these fully avoidable deaths took place, our country has embraced a new form of tyranny, one unblessed by this thought: *Today, if a person feels strongly about some issue, he mistakenly thinks his cause is bolstered by the heightened strength of his emotion.* It is not, since arguments are made, and won or lost, based on sound and logical reason, not emotional pitch or fever.

Therefore, a tyranny of liberation, 'La liberazione', has ensued. Let us use for the moment the Italian word for this fake freedom. Let us study this word by itself in the context of these three men's deaths.

Since they have gone, and I would make the case, and because they have so hatefully gone away, the rules have changed. Thus, we no longer speak of 'Fellow citizens' and mean it. We are no longer united, together; rather, starting with those three senseless deaths, we have fractured ourselves apart, breaking into 1000 different pieces, like a precious ceramic vase that has fallen from the high mantle above the fireplace and crashed onto the tile floor.

I maintain that their passings have helped to engender this regrettable Cultural Revolution. Had they lived, conditions within our culture would not be as bad, catastrophic, and as confusing as they are today. Take manners: Mostly gone they are now, especially in certain, chip-on-the shoulder parts of the country. Some must have already concluded: Now that they are gone, why be civil? At one point and another, all three men urged restraint, caution, judiciousness. Where are those things now? Everywhere kindness is depleted, discourse is heavily coarsened, and real, respectful debate is rare.

Look at all that has been accepted as normal or glamorous since that most fractious, false, and mean decade of the 60s took place, those years when I was finishing up high school. Let us create a sad list and call it 'The Lamentable List of Seven':

1. Abortion,
2. Drug use,
3. The Sexual Revolution,
4. Corruption, pervasive if unseen, at all levels of government,
5. Over-riding lack of excellence at every level of education,
6. Political Correctness, and perhaps most crucially,
7. God's death.

I do not comprehend how all these things so quickly and so blithely took place and were absorbed, accepted, as it overnight, with nary a dissent, hardly a probing question, scarcely a word of rebellion.

One must ask: Would our three deceased men have supported or countenanced these unfortunate and harmful trends? Would they not have instantly pointed out the manifold negative aspects necessarily attached to each one of them?

For instance, would they not have stressed the importance of fidelity in the family? Would they not have explained the harmfulness of unknown drugs? Would they not have delineated the ongoing calamity of abortion? Would they not have demanded tougher schools and teachers who compel learning? Would they not have demanded honest government? Would they not have called for free discourse instead of the stifling of political correctness? And would they not have praised and saluted God, instead of touting His demise?

Let us make a list of pertinent questions:

1. How was abortion so quickly accepted?
2. Why was cocaine not derived as dangerous since it harms the heart, replaces pleasure centers in the brain, and reshuffles the psyche?
3. What if all men acted like Hugh Hefner or does that sort of strict logic no longer pertain?
4. When we know that corruption is ubiquitous, why is it tolerated?
5. Why do we encourage rising salaries and benefits for the educational elites, when test scores only decline?

6. Do we not know that when free speech is stifled, the future of the republic is in doubt?

7. How precisely does one know, without question of glimpse of doubt, that God is dead? Where is the needed proof?

Today, due to this lassitude and laziness, our national discourse is impossibly worsened. No one is attentive to the other's view! Inflexibility reigns. Both sides shout and yell, never having learned to listen, to debate, even to pause. The 'gentle art of conversation' has disappeared as quietly as, I have read, the Browns left St. Louis to become the Orioles. The year was 1954, and I was less than three years old that spring, so I do not remember that migration. I cannot leave baseball for long.

Thus, today, absent the civilizing and fine guidance of these three men, their patience and forbearance, our country is split apart, cleaned in two halves like never before except, perhaps, for those five long years of the Civil War. We think more about what separates us than what joins us. Who can argue that we are not as a people, as a nation, not splintering, fracturing, and falling apart? And, if that is, indeed, an unfortunate case, is it not time to stop the breaking apart, the shattering, this disintegration of the national will?

In the meantime, while we decide if we still wish to squabble with each other, maybe we ought to get back to the basics, to recall my dad's quotations from Coach John Wooden (who passed away, ironically, exactly when I first wrote these words); again, here are his surprisingly simple diction: Don't lie. Don't cheat. Don't steal. Don't moan. Don't complain. Don't be a victim. As his excellent and rambunctious red-haired center, Bill Walton, said just the other day on the radio,

"That covers 85% of the issues in life."

My dad implied so many years ago that if a person followed these rules, he would become strong, not weak. Is it not good to be strong? Yet, now, more and more, we have become weak, ninnies, sissies, pansies, or what Ken Kesey calls 'Sissy shits' in the movie, Sometimes A Great Notion (1971), always asking government to do more, even though to do so is economically untenable, making us spoiled moaning and groaning entitlement babies, and well beyond a mere or temporary petulance.

Maybe Coach Wooden was smart after all! I suggest that if all through these years if we had been following his most sage advice, we would not be in such a pickle today, always acting entitled.

Today, if we watch television news shows and base our conclusions only on that observance, we will quickly conclude that we hate each other. And yet, all of us know that hate only brings unhappiness. And that is what Robert Kennedy knew when he delivered his Aeschylus speech in Indiana. He knew what must be done, the divine and magical healing that must take place.

I think now we may have too much time to watch our own souls. Better: To let them soar about, unwatched. (Re: Heinrich Heine; 1797–1856) We must regard them less. God tells me how to request His grace and to see His visage in others, but only if I listen to Him and not to myself.

We have here on our soiled hands some blood, because we killed these three decent men. These three guys weren't tin-pot, no-count woofers from Pittsburgh, or lazy wheats, or crappy paperhangers from Kansas; rather, they were the foremost moral leaders for that decade in America. And we killed them all. Thus, it is no surprise that we have a growing crisis upon our struggling souls; yet, since it is of our own making, it may be solved by our own hands. I fear, sometimes, that every day by inaction or paralysis, we make it a little worse, tighten the noose a little more closely around our shrinking necks. Instead, if we were to start again in the beginning, before the clouds may settle, to return to where we once were, before these assassinations took place, to commence a new and unfettered life away from the devil's ropes, to go back to that time when we helped a neighbor because he needed it. Above all, we must chase happiness less. Nonetheless, though wants and joys, we must ply onward and always looking up to God for direction and strength.

Yes, you may well say,

"Preposterous, your premise is foolish, that these three men might have stemmed us away from the unmistakable cultural slide."

Granted, granted; but they would have helped, assuaged, lessened its harmful effects, and too, since all three were very intelligent, they would have pointed out the unintended negative consequences of this or that. They would have pushed us away from so much of the inevitable corruption within our government that has taken place, the ugly degradation of our culture, and the full embrace of vice. These three extremely gifted men, by both word and example, promoted civility, kindness, and strength through toughness, thus forming a composite moral compass. Parroting John Donne, all three understood that,

"No man is an island entire onto himself," and that all people are knitted together in ineffable ways that are difficult to delineate and explain. They would have realized, to use that word for the very first time, the deleterious consequences of abortion, for example, and all the other fake cultural flavors of the month.

Since all three men are gone, we do not rightly know whose war to fight nor what king to follow. If we had not killed them, perhaps we would have followed them. In which case, would our world not be vastly different than the chaotic and weakened mess we see today?

In conclusion (Pfui! It's about the merciful time they gave this Percy boy pitcher the hook. The snow job idiota has been thrown nothing but grounders for fuddy hours! But, yet again, can there ever be too many words used to discuss the issues? Can there?), let us briefly and specifically consider each of these three men for the last time, and exactly how their assassinations colored our new and now always-growing social disorder, and what each of them might have brought to a world which is now too dark to see itself clearly.

Because of his dutiful observances of the pre-World War II years in Britain, John Kennedy knew that all societies have an arc or slope; that is to say, they build themselves and then they crumble. He saw, however, the best and brightest (e.g., Stanley Baldwin during his last term as Great Britain's Prime Minister from 1935 to 1937) urge that Hitler, despite his obvious menace, be accommodated, placated, and given what he wanted. However, here one word comes to mind: Czechoslovakia. John Kennedy understood that often, no, usually, cultures over time become weak and decadent. That has been, and as a historian, he would have grasped it, the world's story.

Also, I suspect that in his mind he understood that the communists could not be beaten in Vietnam, and that that same battle (really an outgrowth of the indeterminist end to World War II) might be better joined somewhere else. Upon his re-election in 1964, had he lived, many students of his presidency suggest he would have scaled back our involvement there. Had he won that election, he would have felt less constrained by political influences. And all that mayhem and social upheaval, the corruption and the loss of life on both sides would have been avoided.

Because John Kennedy was so often ill, stretching back to his teens in the 30s, so frequently confined to bed, he read much and deeply, usually in histories and biographies; and, therefore, of our three men, he probably possessed the sharpest mind, the keenest intellect. He was always asking himself,

"Why this? Why not that? What is the downside if we pursue this course? Have you considered all the possible results stemming from your advice?"

And I maintain, going back to our 'List of Seven', going from abortion's easy acceptance to the arrogant pronouncement of God's death, that he would have fought against all seven. But, since we killed him, we shall never know for sure what he might have said and what he might have done.

Finally, who did it? Who or what killed President Kennedy that awful day in Dallas? After the Bay of Pigs fiasco in April of 1961, he knew that the Central Intelligence Agency was keenly focused against him, especially since the president was turning away from the conflict in South Vietnam. Angry and feeling as if he had been stabbed in the back by the agency, Kennedy famously vowed to break the agency into a thousand pieces. My gut tells me that the CIA committed the evil dead, and that it is still covering up the crime today, sixty years later, even though, sooner or later, everyone knows everything. The former head of the CIA, Allen W. Dulles, was fired by Kennedy in November of 1961 for his nefarious hand in the flawed invasion, yet, remarkably, that same man, Dulles, was put in charge of the Warren Commission charged with investigating the assassination. I think that situation is aptly described as,

"The foxes minding the chicken coop."

The truth is our government for many decades has treated us like we are children, and we are dumb and docile enough to allow that continual transgression to take place.

Martin Luther King, Jr., as a preacher's son himself, possessed a deeply spiritual core. He understood the idea that we are, at base, primarily moral beings. Throughout his abbreviated life, he did the right and timely thing in fighting for the slighted rights of the black man. Whenever he preached, before some Southern cracker killed him, he exposed the traditional values: Charity, faith, love. He spoke for fidelity within marriage. He would have railed against the sexual revolution and the rampant promiscuity that it promotes. He would have looked at the near-complete disintegration of the black family since the

60s and been rightly and vociferously appalled. Dr. King would have been disgusted by the very high rate of black unwed mothers. He would preach,

"Is it any wonder that black society has devolved into such chaos? Knock it off! Behave! Find one beautiful black woman and be faithful to her. Give her your whole heart and only then will you be saved."

Seeing that in so many quarters, black male promiscuity is praised, extolled, encouraged, for the remainder of his life, Dr. King would have combated that harmful and corrosive promiscuity. That debate would have been a testy war, but since he was a good soldier, he would have been ready for the fight.

Yet, to me, it is particularly sad, gnawing, and distasteful that Robert Kennedy was killed. With his grit and mettle, because of his broad spiritual expansion with 'the dark night of the soul' after Jack's death and due to his plucky, never-failing Irish tenacity and sense of humor (something today's dour politicians could use more of), perhaps he would have been the best of all. As before stated, (but worth re-stating) because of his brother's ugly death, Robert Kennedy had to reach out beyond this pale and disordered earth, to ask for God's grace, so that with it he might continue to live beyond that death with, it is to be hoped, a slowly diminishing grief. That process made him stronger, better, tougher, more resilient; in short, it made him a better leader, for, if he could survive that cruelest of events, he would have been able to get through anything else. Therefore, he could have survived and vanquished any problem that ruling our country might have presented to him. Thus, his death, for me, is especially vexing and troubling. Now we can only guess what might have been.

As a president, he would have been charitable and a pain-in-the-ass at the same time, Zeus and Francis (yes, his middle name) conjoined. He, as a father of eleven children, would have contested if not mocked the constant emasculation of males that today so marks our culture. He would have told some members of the feminist movement who promote weak manhood or the unimportance of a father,

"Go find a man to love, if you can do so."

He would have mocked our entitlement society and said to us all,

"We can do better. Much better. Now, get to work."

With his pluck and never-failing Irish determination, with little doubt he would have been one of our better presidents.

As I sat in that television room so many years ago now, watching the dreary details of his murder unfold, my wet and muddy orchard boots still dripping dirt and water onto the floor, I knew much of this instantly, instinctively, even though I could not say it out loud. I knew it in the same way that a tiring pitcher knows that a strapping hitter, probably an outfielder but perhaps some speedy galoot from the hot corner, 3rd, is about to get a hit, and not some wimpy-ass Texas Leaguer either. And all of this goes through the pitcher's frightened mind even before the batter strides to the plate.

Robert Kennedy would have prospered and exalted in the role. Because of his history, because of what cruelties fate had had in store for him and his family, he would have asked of himself, proposed only the deepest, most probing questions, and grown in fullest wisdom in that action. It all would have been quite something spectacular to see, and then, later, to study. Might he have been our own benign despot? Yes. Yes. It is more than a convenient folly for us to think so, since, after all his training and suffering, his spiritual growth, he would have been simply meant for the job. Robert Kennedy would have been a masterful president, and one always growing on the job. He had gone through all the conditioning, all the difficulties and trials, and he would have run the entire long length of the Indians' gauntlet, so then it would have been time to play the game. And, from time to time, alert like any good coach, he would have said to us many things, delivering many imperative commands to his charges, ones which we would have needed to hear, among them:

"We must stop fighting against each other now. Don't you understand that we are all knitted together as part of the family of man?

"Like an athlete, we must always make ourselves stronger. Stronger! And we must occasionally sacrifice for others with no expectation of gain.

"Do you care? Are you committed? Do the right thing!

"Are we what FDR used to call weaklings or playboys, or what? When will we learn not to trifle with God? When?

"Damn your extravagant wishes and desires. They are simply enslavements, every one of them. Do what must be done. And go do it now!

"Can you remember all this? Are you going to forget these commands and suggestions? Are you?"

9 798888 101307